The Wolf's
PURSUIT

By

Rachel Van Dyken

The Wolf's Pursuit
London Fairy Tales, Book 3
by Rachel Van Dyken
Blue Tulip Publishing

Second Edition

THE WOLF'S PURSUIT
Copyright © 2014 RACHEL VAN DYKEN
ISBN 13 978-1502331984
ISBN 1502331985
Cover art designed by P.S. Cover Design

PROLOGUE

SHE LOVED FLOWERS — the pink frilly ones that made a man roll his eyes in disgust. Yet Hunter could not bring himself to deny her anything. She was his soul mate, his love. And after being married for a year, he could no longer manage being apart from her. The life of a spy was unapologetic. Hunter would be gone for weeks at a time, spending many sleepless nights tossing and turning, aching for Lucy, the Royal Duchess of Haverstone.

Knowing he lacked the maturity of romance, given his young age of one-and-twenty, he had poured countless hours into this meeting, into her surprise.

He crossed the street and smiled, thinking of the way she would throw her head back in laughter and leap into his arms. Never a conventional bride, she didn't care a whit about propriety and often kissed him in public, much to the ton's dismay.

He wanted one of her kisses now. Needed to taste her lips.

Hunter pulled out his pocket-watch and examined the

numbers. A tad late; he had spent a ridiculous amount of time picking out her favorite flowers and daydreaming on the way to their meeting place.

As he crossed the final street to Gunther's, he watched as Lucy waved wildly in the other direction. She raised both hands high above her head, frantically aiming for someone's attention. He picked up his pace. Anticipation overtook him as he watched his tiny wife begin to jump up and down. Something must be truly exciting for her to be acting so rashly. Truthfully, her behavior was reminiscent of when she saw him for the first time after being away for weeks.

And then, she stomped her tiny foot and began marching across the street.

Alarmed, he began to run.

But it was too late.

The carriage was moving too fast. She looked to her left just in time to see the carriage jolting out of the way, but not enough.

She fell to the ground.

Hunter swore. His legs felt like lead as he screamed and ran to her side. Blood trickled from her mouth. Her petite body was bent in an unnatural angle. Tears streamed down his face into his mouth. The taste of salt was revolting, for it reeked of her death.

"Lucy, love, can you hear me? Everything is going to be fine, just fine." He grasped her lifeless hand. She tried to shake her head. "Don't move, just lie still. I love you. I love you so much."

A single tear ran down her face. "I l-love you." Voice hoarse and weak, her lips trembled as she tried again to speak. Breath came out in short gasps.

"No, stay with me, you can't leave me, Lucy! Do you understand? You can't! You just can't." Hunter's tears clouded his vision but not enough, for the last thing he saw was her blue eyes turn lifeless as her chest heaved its last breath.

"No, no!" Hunter wailed, not caring that he was still in the middle of the street. His body trembled. Surely this was a nightmare that he would wake up from! The flowers in his hand, the anniversary flowers, were never meant to cover her grave.

Strong hands grasped his chest, pulling him away from the street. He heard a voice barking orders and looked up into the eyes of his twin brother.

Eyes that held guilt, shame, and remorse. "She thought I was you. I didn't know, I didn't..." Ash's eyes held unshed tears. "I was too late. I didn't know. Oh, what have I done?" Ash's face was pale and haunted as he embraced his brother.

Hunter was unable to say anything. No words would come, nothing. He felt lifeless, an empty void. And he knew, without a doubt, that he would forever remember this day, not purely because the love of his life had died in his arms, but because in her death she had taken his very soul with her.

Never would he be the same.

CHAPTER ONE

Red—

The Office would like you to please hand over the information you obtained from Napoleon. Failure to do so will result in the end of your life. I would love nothing more than to wrap my claws around the neck of the one woman able to best me.

Yours truly,

—Wolf

Nine years later
February 1815, Belgium, 30 miles away from Waterloo

HUNTER WOLFBANE, ROYAL DUKE of Haverstone, was in a foul mood. His horse had run off after yet another gunshot had narrowly missed Hunter's head, leaving him with no food, no drink, and worst of all, no whiskey.

How was he to make his way around the frigid countryside without his whiskey? It had taken him two days tramping through the melting snow to reach the village near Dominique Maksylov's estate, where he was staying.

As a spy for the Crown, Hunter had felt it his duty to notify Wellington that French soldiers were still in the vicinity and openly attacking civilians. His horse had done the job of getting him to Wellington's camp in record time and then promptly ran off the next morning when Hunter had stopped to stretch his legs. Blasted Russian horses.

Duty done. All he wanted was a hot bath, a supple wench, and new boots so his feet could get some respite. After all, without his horse he had resorted to trudging through the melting snow like some common criminal.

The inn was only a few more steps. Already he could taste the warm bread on his tongue, the ale pouring down his throat, the soft willing woman beneath him—

And then something struck him.

Not a thought, though it may have been equally shocking to have logical thought after being so famished.

No. It was something smaller.

But sharp.

And then another one hit.

"What the devil?" Who in the blazes was pelting him with rocks! His eyes adjusted to the glaring landscape as the sun peeked through the branches of the trees.

Nothing.

There was no one within his vicinity.

So, this was what it was like to go mad? Truthfully, he'd known that one day his past would catch up with him. After all, one could only lie and manipulate so many times in the name of His Majesty before he forgot the truth of his existence.

Resigned to his fate, he continued his walk toward the inn.

A rock sailed into the side of his face.

He hadn't expected madness to hurt this much. Nor for it to be as realistic as the blood currently trickling down his cheek.

He muttered a curse and took another look around him. All he saw was melting snow, dingy buildings, a woman digging up...

Wait. His eyes went back to the woman. A smile curved his lips as he stuffed his hands in his pockets and walked over to where she was digging. Bum in the air, and curse words escaping her mouth quite like a sailor at war. He smugly waited.

Finally, as rocks and dirt continued to soar, she stopped and kicked the ground.

"Looking for something?" *Your mind perhaps; you've lost it?*

The woman ceased her incessant digging and paused only momentarily to glare at him. To be fair, he deserved that and far worse, considering his eyes were naturally trained on her bum as it was in the air at that precise moment.

Blushing profusely, the girl put her hands on her hips, dirt clumps making her dress all the more blemished, and sighed. "What do you want?"

"What do I want?" Hunter repeated. "Well, that all depends, I guess. You see, it's been a while since I've answered such an open-ended question, but considering my lack of food or drink, I think I shall start with the biggest desire." He cleared his throat. "You see that inn over there? I want to find myself smothered beneath a buxom lady, preferably while inebriated with whiskey, and perhaps if I am being particularly selfish, I want to eat bread, lots and lots of warm bread. But firstly, what I want, nay what I desire, is that you stop pelting me with rocks."

"The only lady residing at the inn will not only smother you within an inch of your life, but dribble meat on your person while doing so, but by all means, experience it for yourself." She smiled sweetly, managed a curtsy, and continued her digging.

Another rock hit his boot. The chit spoke in perfect German, which should have been frightening, considering it had been a great while since Hunter had spoken the language. He cleared his throat again and tried, "Perhaps if you tell me what you're digging for? I can be of service and be on my way."

"Or you can just be on your way now," she said through gritted teeth.

"Allow me this small boon; after all, now my curiosity is piqued." *As well as my lust*, his brain added as he was again given quite a nice view of her feminine curves.

"My pistol." Her hands dug deeper into the earth. "I buried it last night, and now I cannot find it!"

Several thoughts went through Hunter's head at that moment, the first and most obvious being what the devil she was doing with a pistol? The second, why, if she needed the pistol so desperately, was she set on burying it?

"Did it die? Was it in need of a proper burial then? It seems you buried it at least a foot down. How can the poor thing breathe with that much earth hovering above it?"

She stopped. "If I tell you, will you leave me alone?"

Well, that was rude. "Perhaps."

"I'm going to rescue my sister. She's trapped in that dratted castle by the Beast, and I need my pistol in order to retrieve her!"

"So why the devil did you bury it?" Hunter ignored the information, thinking it nothing but an exaggeration. The only woman Dominique had been successful in capturing was Isabelle, and she was by no means trapped, nor was she German. Obviously this raven-haired beauty was a touch mad.

"I couldn't very well conceal it, not when all my belongings were stolen, and it cannot fit in my corset. As you can well see, considering you've been staring at my body like a dog in heat for the past five minutes!"

7

Blast, she was beautiful when provoked. Her soft white skin had a touch of pink on her cheeks that perfectly matched her cherry red lips.

"Am I to understand that you are here, in this place, trying to find your pistol, so you can shoot the Beast and rescue your sister?"

"Yes, I believe that is what I just said."

"Well, this day has just gotten brighter. I say!" Hunter clapped his hands in amusement. "Allow me to accompany you to the castle. I would love nothing more than to see the look on the Beast's face while he stares down the barrel of a pistol. Been meaning to challenge the fellow to a duel for years now!" Hunter couldn't believe his good luck. He had needed something to amuse him after such a long journey. Perhaps he could keep her, as a sort of... pet. He smiled at the thought.

"You'll take me there, and not hinder me?" the girl asked skeptically, as her brow lifted.

"Absolutely. In fact, I may just take a shot myself. After all, I'm sure he deserves it. For taking... what did you say your sister's name was?"

"Isabelle," she said in perfect English.

Blazes. This was turning out to be the best day of his life! "You don't say?" Hunter grinned, slowly approached the girl, and offered his arm. "And what may I call you, dear lady?"

"Gwen. Apologies for using German. I thought perhaps it best I hid my identity. I've seen far too many French soldiers scattered about."

Smart girl. Now there was an interesting turn of events. Beautiful, smart, and violent. "Right, well, allow me at least a few minutes of respite, a hot meal, and we'll be on our way. Agreed?"

"Fine." She accepted his arm. "But only because I am without a weapon and cannot possibly take the man on myself."

"No, you'd most likely die." Hunter nodded, trying to make himself sound more useful, though he knew Dominique could very well handle a mad female. It was of no matter. Once she saw her sister was healthy and content, he would ask to keep her. Gwen, after all, couldn't very well travel alone without being ruined. The poor thing was probably already compromised, for what girl trudged from England to the continent by herself? One that had no reputation to protect, or not one to speak of. Truly, it was the beginning of a wonderful day.

They walked in silence until they reached the inn. Upon entering, Hunter felt on edge. And it had nothing to do with the girl next to him. She was distracting to a dangerous level, and it took everything within him to peel his eyes away from her as he ordered food and drink.

No, the prickling on the back of his neck had everything to do with the men sitting in the far corner. English gentlemen. He could spot one a mile away; after all, he was one of them, though he'd been spying for the Crown for the past ten years and had yet to re-enter into society since his wife's death.

He shuddered at the thought. He never allowed himself to think of her, not in that way, with her broken body and blood trickling out of her mouth. The faint smile on her lips as her eyes went cold.

Ale, he needed ale.

Out of habit, he put a protective arm around Gwen. They sat in the corner so he could have a better view of the rest of the establishment. It was not common to see any Englishmen in the area so close to the action. If they were here, they were soldiers, and he knew every able-bodied spy.

The tavern wench approached, completely blocking his view, for she was at least twice his size, and not in a flattering way. His eyes skimmed where she loomed over him, which he hoped she wouldn't take as an invitation, and slowly drew up to her face. Merciful heavens, she had a mustache. He opened his mouth to speak and then closed it again.

"So the fancy gent likes what he sees, does he?" She winked.

Blast. He'd take the French any day. They'd probably win the war if they had women like this working for them. But his eyes, devil take it, he could not avert his eyes from her face. Almost like she was casting some witch's spell on him. Out of desperation he reached for Gwen's hand.

Gwen giggled. "Sorry, my husband here hasn't slept a wink since we've been married. Just yesterday, if you get my meaning. Would you mind terribly getting us some ale and fresh bread? We'll be taking a rest here at the inn tonight."

The woman flashed one last grin at Hunter before leaving.

He shuddered. "I assure you I've never in my life been without words until now."

Gwen removed her hand from his death grip and sighed. "Well, at least I know you're not a spy. With manners like that, you'd surely get yourself killed. You cannot simply gawk at a woman like that. It isn't done, and now you've shown weakness. Don't trust me to save you. I sure hope you can hold your own with the Beast tomorrow."

If she only knew. "I'll manage, though things may go better if I simply stand behind you."

"Coward."

"Absolutely not, it just provides a better view."

"I'm sorry, rake seems to be the word."

"Thank you," Hunter said warmly, and added, "wife" with a saucy grin.

"I did that only to help you, not because I want any sort of attachment. You should know that if I hadn't done so, that tavern wench would be at this very moment smothering you with—"

"—please, I hope to keep my appetite."

Gwen smiled sweetly and winked.

Blast, where had this woman fallen from? Heaven? Every mannerism bespoke a cunning intelligence he'd never before seen in polite society. Not that he would truly know, since he'd been everywhere but London since… *the incident.*

He cleared his throat and looked away as a knot lodged itself uncomfortably in his chest.

The doors to the establishment opened up. Two impeccably dressed men walked in, making their way directly for the Englishmen.

Gwen squinted in their direction, then looked back to Hunter. "Strange."

"What?" He tried to play innocent of the whole situation, though it was indeed odd.

"Oh, it's probably nothing."

"Enlighten me, I've been alone without whiskey or horse for a day now. I do so love to be entertained."

Gwen exhaled and leaned in. "See those two men who just walked in?"

"Yes." Of course he had; he was a spy, after all.

"Just yesterday I was on the same ship as them."

Hunter leaned even further forward. "And this is significant because?"

"Well, it could be nothing." Gwen craned her head to look at the men and then looked back at Hunter. "But they were speaking French."

"And returning from?"

"London. I heard them saying they had business with the Earl of Trehmont."

Hunter cursed without realizing he was giving himself away. Everyone knew Trehmont was without funds. He'd worked for the War Office nearly as long as Hunter. What would the French want with Trehmont?

He cleared his throat and strained to listen to their conversation.

The men ordered ale and toasted.

Nothing all that strange, except...

They toasted to winning the war. And the Englishmen grinned in agreement. Money was then exchanged. Enraged, Hunter gripped the side of the table and tried to steady his breathing. What the devil was going on?

"Codes," one man said as he slid a scrap of paper across the table to one of the Frenchmen. "I think you will be pleased with what you see."

The man grinned and lifted up the paper. "And our man is in position?"

"He is." The Englishman nodded. "Though his price just doubled."

The Frenchman sneered. "On what grounds?"

The Englishman leaned forward. "The codes are unbreakable. Surely you realize how fortune shines upon you at this very moment?"

"Fine." The Frenchman took a long swig of ale and then chuckled. "It has been a pleasure doing business with your... employer."

Every muscle in Hunter's body tightened. "Listen." He grabbed Gwen's hand. "This is very important; do you understand?"

She pulled back, but nodded.

"I need you to spend the night with me."

"Pardon?" Her voice carried a bit too loudly for his tastes. The tavern wench apparently overheard, because she seemed extremely disappointed as she put down the bread and ale.

"I need you to truly pretend to be my wife, and we need to stay the night. I need to search their room." It wasn't the most brilliant plan he had come up with, but a man staying on his own was a man watched. If they looked married, then the men wouldn't pay attention to him.

"Because?" Gwen giggled. "What, are you a spy or something? Truly, does the War Office take everyone these days?" Uncontrollable mirth washed over her as she placed her hands on the table and threw her head back and laughed even harder.

He would have been amused.

If the exact line of her throat and sound of her laugh hadn't reminded him of Lucy.

Suddenly angry, he stood up and grabbed her by the arm, hauling her toward the innkeeper. "We need a room for the night." His grip tightened on her arm, but she said nothing.

The innkeeper nodded.

"And please, bring us a light supper along with some more ale to our room. We are on our honeymoon, after all."

He slipped the innkeeper enough money for Gwen to begin to choke.

"My wife." Hunter nodded to Gwen.

The innkeeper shook his head in understanding. "Of course, and your name?"

"Maksylov," Hunter lied, though he knew it was rare for Dominique the Beast to go into the village. The innkeeper wouldn't be able to tell the two of them apart and Dominique practically owned the place, so truly it would matter not. Besides, he'd just given the man enough blunt to stay in business for the remaining year.

The innkeeper grabbed a key and led them up the stairs.

Gwen was quiet.

Until the door shut.

Then all havoc broke loose.

With a cry she stomped on his foot and reached for the door, but he slammed it in place and locked it.

"Who are you?" She pushed him against the door, which

truthfully felt quite good, considering he'd been without any sort of female companionship for what felt like years. Perhaps it had only been a few weeks, days even, but she felt good, so soft and delicate.

He wrapped his arms tightly around her, then grabbed the back of her head and pulled her in for a kiss. Only meaning for it to be quick, he was quite surprised when she opened her mouth in response, after little coaxing. Her mouth was hot and tasted of ale, her tongue like velvet as it massaged his.

Who needed whiskey when he had Gwen? With a moan, he loosened his hold on her and reached for her face, needing to drink in more of her.

As his hands touched that perfect ivory skin, he felt the cold blade of a knife against his throat. "I said, who are you?" The steel edged deeper into his skin, blood began to trickle down his neck, but it could have been water for all he cared. Stunned, he could only watch her eyes darken. A haunting look passed between them both.

And he knew.

It was the eyes, for they were the windows to the soul, were they not? Filled with anguish, pain, bitterness, and yes, guilt.

Her very eyes reflected his own, for only two types of people in the world carried such a heaviness within them. Those who have had innocent blood on their hands too many times to count, or those who have loved and lost everything important to them.

He wondered which she was.

With a flick of his wrist, faster than she could respond, Hunter manipulated her hand, causing the knife to clamor to the floor.

They stood, face to face, breathing heavily. He assessed her coolly, calculating each movement of her face, noticing her pupils as they dilated and her nostrils flared, only for her to stare back with unwavering strength.

"I'm a spy," they said at the same time.

Gwen lifted an eyebrow and moved to walk past him. "Well, you aren't a very good one."

Amused, Hunter threw out his foot, tipped her over it, sending her sprawling into his arms. He held her hands high above her head as he leaned in close to her face. "Darling, I'm the best."

Her chest heaved with exertion. "Impossible. The Wolf is the best, everyone knows that. And you cannot possibly be him."

"Alright." Perhaps he could escape without giving her his identity, without compromising himself or her. With a sigh, he dropped her to the floor and marched over the wash basin to clean the blood from his neck. "And your name?"

"Gwen."

Hunter laughed, bracing a hand on either side of the basin as he leaned forward, allowing the water droplets to splash into the bowl. "Not your real name, love. The one you go by when you're out spreading your legs for God and country."

With a scream, she lunged for him, as expected, for no man could insult a woman in that way and not expect some sort of bloodshed. Patiently, he waited until she was seconds away from removing his head. Then he jolted to the side, elbowed her in the back, causing her to curse and stumble.

She kicked him hard in the stomach as she went down, then flipped onto her back and pulled his body toward hers, again holding the knife to his neck. Blast, and he had just cleaned himself up. Well, now they were just wasting time.

"Your name, if you don't mind," Hunter ground out through clenched teeth. It was deuced hard, trying to keep his arousal in check. The blasted woman had drawn him to his knees twice within ten minutes, and he'd be lying if he said he didn't want her.

A surge of pride stormed her eyes, making them widen for just a second before indifference returned. "Red, I go by Red."

Hunter was silent.

Quite a bad habit to suddenly develop.

He cleared his throat. "As in the very Red who was able to infiltrate the highest ranks of Napoleon's trusted elite and gain secrets that even the Wolf could not obtain, and all within the first month of employ?"

"The very one."

"I don't believe you." But truly, he did. Mainly because he was ready to spill his entire life story based solely on the fact that she was the only woman who had ever used violence on him.

He found it wildly arousing.

"It is more believable than you being the Wolf." Her laugh echoed within the room. Pride taking another huge blow, he almost blurted out his identity for a second time, but thought better of it. After all, if she truly did not know him, then that would mean it would be reasonable for him to experiment. After all, there was enough sexual tension in that room to make a vicar sin.

"Then I guess I truly am the worst spy," he purred into her ear, minding the steel flexing against his neck. "After all, you were the one who noticed the men on the ship as well as the men in the inn. You truly must be the notorious Red. An honor, I assure you."

"The pleasure's all mine," she said breathlessly as her grip on the knife loosened. Beginner's mistake, for it was all the chance he was going to get.

Seduction, for Hunter, had always been simple, a strategic battle plan of sorts. Make her desire him, mirror that desire, compliment, touch, please, and finally leave. After all, he was always starving after such an encounter, and it was always best to keep all seductions and encounters under twelve hours.

Always.

His hand moved to her neck. Closing his eyes he breathed in the scent of her skin. A spicy mix of cinnamon and honey. His thumb rubbed her bottom lip. A pink tongue snuck out and licked playfully at his thumb. Gwen's eyes darkened.

And he had her.

Precisely where he and other parts of his anatomy wanted her.

On her back.

And at his mercy.

She didn't even see the pistol slip out of his pocket, for he had already knocked her cold by the time her eyes widened in realization.

He lifted her onto the bed and cursed. "Worst spy in the history of the Crown? I think not." She would wake up within the hour, cursing him to perdition, but he would be long gone, never to see her again.

But before he left, he had a little spying to do. Spying that even Red couldn't accomplish without getting her pretty little self shot.

Without another thought to the woman lying in the bed, Hunter left to sneak into the Englishmen's rooms. After handing the innkeeper some blunt, he was extremely helpful in giving Hunter the information he needed as to the rooms rented to the men.

After five minutes of picking the lock, he was finally able to make it into the first room. Nothing. It was as if the gentleman hadn't brought a thing with him on the trip.

He tried the next three.

All empty.

Cursing, he made his way down the stairs. The chairs where the gentlemen had been sitting were empty. Money left on the table.

They'd left. The inn had been a front.

Hunter cursed again and made his way to the front door, only to see it burst open. A Norse-looking fellow barged in, demanding to know where a certain English girl named Gwen had disappeared to. If Hunter hadn't been so tired after fighting off the wench, he'd have the good sense to be alarmed that an Englishman was boldly yelling such incriminating things about the girl.

"How dare that strong-willed defiant child leave home!" the duke screamed, "Selfish, selfish woman!"

Hunter lifted a brow at the man's words, her reputation truly was well and ruined by now.

Either she was his wife or a family member. Judging by the wild look in the man's eyes, Hunter assumed she must be his sister. For any man with even an ounce of pride would not announce to perfect strangers that he was not man enough to keep his wife happy in his bedroom.

The man continued to yell at the innkeeper. The money Hunter had given the innkeeper had been sufficient it seemed, considering he had to be lying through his teeth.

Poor sod, he was going to get his ears boxed if Hunter didn't intervene.

With a quick shake of his head, his hair fell wildly about his face. He limped heavily toward the Englishman and winced. Cursing as if he was in pain from a war injury but too foxed to realize why. A large black coat was left on a nearby chair, and he quickly put it over his shoulders. Hunter stopped in front of the Englishman and scowled. "Gwen, you say?"

His words were purposefully slurred.

"Yes," the man clipped. His eyes narrowed fiercely as he clenched his teeth together.

"I believe she's already been found, just up there in that room." Hunter pointed to where he had left her, but made sure to keep his head low as to not give away his identity. "Some spy was boasting about how he rescued her from certain ruin, as well as getting herself shot! Can you believe she was spouting out nonsense that some Beast had stolen her sister? Truthfully, if this very capable and well known — and let's not forget infamous — spy, the Wolf, hadn't stumbled across her, she may have very well been killed, or worse ruined, if you get my meaning." Blazes, he forgot to slur. Well, that's what pride did to a man. He winced and toppled to the side, then stole a glance at the man.

The man's gaze turned murderous. Clearly he got the innuendo.

"My thanks," he finally said, reaching into his pocket.

"No payment necessary. I shall truly sleep better this very night, knowing such a diamond of the first water is safe in her..." Hunter blinked innocently. "I'm sorry, old fellow, who did you say you were? What kind of man would I be if I let some fluffy-looking fancy person take advantage of the poor lass?"

"Montmouth."

Blast. If she was his charge, Hunter had half a mind to feel sorry for him. The savage duke had just recently been married to Rosalind Hartwell, who was in fact Gwen and Isabelle's sister. The only way he was even privy to such information was because he had spent the better part of the past two months with the Beast of Russia, whose wife was none other than Isabelle Hartwell. It was rumored that their family was quite mad, or at least used to be. Some sort of curse had befallen them all. But the rumors had been quickly laid to rest after Montmouth married Lady Rosalind. Though Hunter hadn't found it good timing that his best friend Dominique Maksylov, the Beast, had chosen that opportune time to pay off the family and take Isabelle for his own. The entire sordid tale of that family was one fit for the storybooks or at least a Greek play.

He shook his head. These were the type of theatrics Hunter wanted no part of. Madness? Stealing women? Spies who believed they could do the job of a man? He shuddered and looked at the duke again. "I believe, your grace, that you will find her perfectly unharmed, though quite ruined. Too fancy of a piece and all that. Besides, who knows if she's been alone this whole time or... touched."

Montmouth's gaze narrowed before he bowed his head and lifted his hand to his brow answering gruffly, "I know."

Nodding his thanks, the behemoth of a duke walked to the stairs, and for the second time that day Hunter had an aggravating feeling wash over him, starting from his head and lingering there for a good few seconds before traveling all the way down to his toes.

It was Gwen's fault. And he needed to forget her as soon as possible. *Desperate times*, he thought as he went in search of the wench from earlier. Perhaps she had more ale?

CHAPTER TWO

Dear readers, I'm so eager to be back in town. This Season promises to be one where even wolves are allowed to walk amongst the ton. What, you may wonder, is this author alluding to? None other than the Duke of Haverstone, Hunter Wolfsbane, has been invited back into polite society. He has a reputation far too scandalous for this author to write down, for there are very few words to be found that can describe his level of vulgarity. Let it be advised that debutantes should cease from wearing white. For we know what white reminds wolves of. Sheep. Take care, dear reader, for you do not want any of your little sheep to go astray, not where wolves dare to play. —Mrs. Peabody's Society Papers

Four months later

GWEN GRIPPED HER RETICULE in her hand, most likely making permanent marks on her person as she paced back and forth in the small dusty study. Pieces of light shot in through the drawn curtains. Enough light to see the grim set of Mr. Wilkins' mouth and the heavy concern laden in his brows.

She cleared her throat and took a steadying breath. "Apologies, sir, for my mood. It just seems that there are so many more options than myself. As I explained in my letter, I no longer wish to do this sort of work." There, she'd said it, to his face, no less. Gaining more courage, for she hated letting anyone down, especially the very man who had helped her feed her family before Rosalind married the duke, she managed a small smile and continued. "After all, there are plenty of women working for the Crown. I see no reason for my participating in this, this—"

"Mission," he finished crisply. "It's a mission regardless of how you see it, my lady. If you are quite certain then?" He said it as a question, his speech sounded careless and indifferent, but over the past few months she had grown to know him. He was placating her sense of pride. Curse the man!

"I am certain." But she wasn't. The familiar tick in her blasted gloves began anew, the need to hold a pistol, the way her blood roared when she successfully bested her opponent. No! She could no longer put her family in such danger! Not when both her sisters were so blissfully happy.

Rosalind, her sister, had married the Duke of Montmouth. The man had rode in on his horse quite like a prince, sweeping Rosalind off her feet, or so he said time and time again when his wife wasn't listening.

And Isabelle, well, she had been kidnapped by her husband. Gwen had to admit to finding it terribly romantic. The great Beast of Russia, Dominique Maksylov, was said to possess no heart, yet he proved its existence daily when he doted on Isabelle. His music was currently all the rage throughout the country; a new dance had even been made in their honor.

Isabelle found it taxing and quite embarrassing. Dominique, however, never missed a dance. They had both re-entered into society a few months ago.

Blast. She couldn't even lie to herself in her head. It wasn't just a few months. It had been four months, one day, and by her calculations, four hours. She had done nothing short of jumping out the window, in order to clear her mind of the man who had dared pin her against the wall with his body.

All masculine hardness pressed against her until she'd thought she would expire on the spot. He was cold, heartless, yet so incredibly fearless, it had taken everything in her power to keep her wits about her, especially when he stole a kiss or two.

Pathetic that her first two kisses had been with a spy.

The most notorious spy in all of London.

Infamous rakehell, Hunter, the Wolf. Though to be fair, at the time, she had laughed in his face when he'd shared his identity. It was probably for the best, for it forced the man to put distance between them.

Hours after her meeting, Montmouth had discovered her at the inn, though he knew not of Hunter's identity. Gwen had assumed Hunter to be missing. That is, until days later when they were all happily brought together at Dominique Maksylov's estate, where her sister resided.

Surprise was not the word she would have used to describe the moment. Irritating? Provoking? Yes, those were adequate words, for the first thing Hunter had uttered under his breath when he brought her hand to his lips in a greeting was, "I'll kill you and not blink, if you reveal anything."

Imagine, the nerve of the man! As if she was not currently in the same predicament! She had been working for the Crown for months without her family's knowledge! At the time of her initial dealings with the War Office, she could have walked the streets of London dressed as a footman and her mother wouldn't have batted an eye; granted, it was later decided she was quite mad, but still.

Gwen shook the memories from her head, allowing the feel of the Wolf's kiss to dissolve into her subconscious, though she knew it would be back and she'd yet again want his hands on her, regardless of propriety or the fact that every time he opened his mouth she imagined shooting him with her pistol.

"My lady?" Mr. Wilkins cleared his throat again. "Have you been listening to anything at all? Apologies, but I've never seen you so distracted."

Distracted, hah! Overheated? Well... Gwen gave the man a tight smile. "As I've said before, I no longer wish to endanger myself or my family."

"Alright, well. Off you go."

"Pardon?" Gwen nearly tipped over from the shock. "Aren't you going to try to convince me? Offer me more money? Make me feel guilty for not protecting my country and all that?"

"No." He shook his head. "Good day to you."

"But..."

Mr. Wilkins gave an exasperated sigh. "What is it you want? Do you want me to grovel? For I will not do it. Another agent, the one who is to be your partner, will just have to go at it alone. Not that I doubt his ability to do so, but his cover has long ago been blown, making it increasingly difficult for him to do his job."

"Partner? Another agent?"

"But of course. This was to be a covert operation, my lady. After all, the Season is underway, and the exact place I need you to infiltrate is the one you were born into."

"The Season? You want me to..." Gwen searched for the correct word. "Debut?"

"In a word, yes. But that will be all; I cannot tell you too much, my dear, for you've already said no. The Wolf will no doubt find success sooner without a woman by his side—"

"—I accept!" Gwen shouted.

"What of your family? Hmm? Their safety? Your own personal morals and ethics and..."

Gwen rolled her eyes. She couldn't very well curse her family to perdition, not when she was already certain the Wolf would be there; truly it would be an unkindness to her flesh and blood. Though at this moment, all she cared about was proving to the man that she was his equal as a spy, in every way. "I care for my family a great deal," she said demurely. "However, I am finding the idea that any sort of danger could befall them during the Season appalling, and for that reason, and that alone, I will accept this mission." Well, that reason and the interesting fact that she would be working alongside the man who haunted her dreams every night.

Perhaps she could strangle him in person now that he would be making an appearance.

"Brilliant." Mr. Wilkins grinned. "I'll send word to him posthaste. I just need to iron out a few details with the man. I hope you realize, my lady, that you will be entirely on your own in this operation. The Wolf will be there if you need him, he will provide protection and work as a distraction, but you will be the one to do the dirty work. Do you understand what I am saying?" At Gwen's silence, he continued, "There are some things a woman may do to persuade a man and gain information of a certain type... now do you understand?"

Only too well. For hadn't she done the exact same thing with Napoleon's elite? Only she had been the distraction as the man salivated over her, touched her, and made her feel like a whore. At least now she would have someone to look after her — that is, if the Wolf could keep his paws to himself.

Gwen gave Wilkins a tight smile. "But of course I understand. Good day." He gave her a quick nod, and she walked to the door, her heart pounding, for she finally realized what she had just agreed to.

A debut into society, with none other than the Wolf as her partner. She only hoped she could finish the Season with her wits still intact, and if not that, at least her virginity.

It's easier to believe you're a failure. So much easier than trying to wrap your mind around the simple truth or perhaps the idea that you are so much more than you choose to be.

Growling, Hunter stared down at the papers and sighed. Nine years. It had been nine blasted years since he saw her face, felt her lifeless body in his arms, and not a night went by that he didn't feel the stab of regret slam into his chest.

He should have been on time.

Because when a person has regrets they always go through every other possibility, every outcome, every situation, tossing and turning the puzzle around, trying to make sense of the awful situations that befall them. And Hunter had come to one conclusion, and one conclusion only.

The love of his life, his sun, his moon, his morning star, lost the light in her eyes because he was not but a few minutes late.

Which is why, as he crossed the street into Mayfair that dreary afternoon in London, he felt the need to be early. So early, in fact, that he was able to see the flash of ebony hair as it left the exact place he was to be meeting with Wilkins.

Blast, now he was even seeing Gwen in broad daylight; forget his dreams. The woman was an absolute terror on his peace of mind, and to think, he had only known her for such a short period. To spend more time in her company would be inviting madness right into his life.

And he'd had enough of madness, thank you very much.

With a curse and loud whistle, he thrust his hands into his pockets and marched up the stairs and into the large townhouse.

In the past, he had always let himself in, and often went into the green salon to pour himself a brandy while waiting for Wilkins to finish with his current victim.

If he was lucky, he would barge in on his boss torturing a poor soul for information. Not one to get his hands dirty, Hunter was quite good at delivering empty threats, as well as slicing a man from head to toe without once drawing his knife.

The stale smell of the house was the same as he remembered it.

Always the same.

Hunter cursed, irritated that a smell would cause such melancholy to fall onto his shoulders. He hated when he let his emotions get the best of him. It made him feel like every other sorry idiot out there, just sitting in a room, alone, thinking about the one thing he'd rather die than think about.

He poured himself a brandy and cursed aloud. How was it that, in the time it took for him to take a sip from a glass, everything could change in an instant? How does a person go from smiling to crying? The only obvious answer was that life was not fair. It had never been fair to him. It didn't make sense that within a minute, his smile was replaced with fear, and his joy replaced with tears.

No, life was not fair, and if it was, he certainly wasn't on the receiving end. The brandy sat like a brick in his stomach. Hunter set the glass on the table and rubbed his eyes, the turmoil of the morning getting to him. He needed to stop thinking so much and just get the blasted job done.

Emotions were of no use to him. He laughed bitterly in the empty room. As much as he preached to others about being open and carefree — he was actually quite the opposite of everything he pretended to be.

The sad truth of his ability to laugh through life was based solely on the fact that he didn't care if he lived or died, and that sickened him more than he could bear, for his wife wouldn't have wanted him to live his life in such a way.

But it was the only way he knew to survive.

"Ah, Haverstone, always a pleasure." Wilkins barged into the room, wiping his hands with a cloth.

So it had been dirty business.

Immediately Hunter's mind went to Gwen; had she been involved? Was she still working for the Crown? Had she come to her senses and quit?

"I believe…" Wilkins cleared his throat and took a seat, "that this particular mission may be something you will find…" He looked to the ground and grinned before gazing again at Hunter. "Shall we say, distasteful?"

Hunter tried to appear amused though his mood proved quite the opposite. "Oh? Pray tell, will I need to seduce half of London in the name of the Crown? Perhaps I need only seduce the dingy half, yes?"

"No." Wilkins grinned and leaned back. "Would you care for a brandy?"

"I see." Hunter nodded. Perhaps if he drank more, this sick feeling in his stomach would alleviate. "So it is to be that type of mission."

"But I have not yet explained what it is you need to accomplish."

"You don't need to." Hunter stretched his arms above his head and sighed. "If you find it necessary to give me brandy before the assignment, then it must be nasty business indeed."

Wilkins merely nodded in agreement. After a pregnant silence, he rose from his seat and walked over to the cabinet to pour some brandy. He handed Hunter a glass and threw back the contents of his own before filling it up again.

So it truly was that bad.

"What is it that His Majesty needs me to do?" Hunter asked plainly as he slowly sipped the amber liquid.

"Enter into society." Wilkins winced as he took another sip of brandy. "That is to say, if you can manage it successfully and without seducing the lesser half of London in the process."

Irritated, Hunter drank the rest of the fiery liquid and cursed. "If I can manage? I believe I've been adequately managing for over ten years, Wilkins. Entering into society will be easier than entering into Napoleon's bedroom, I assure you."

"It will not be that easy, *I assure you*." Wilkins fired back.

"Do you so easily forget who I am?"

"No, but clearly you do." Wilkins took a seat opposite Hunter and sighed. "You cannot be absent from society for near a decade after your wife's accident and your brother's mysterious death without causing a debacle. It isn't in the ton's nature and you very well know it. Besides, your cover has long ago been blown, no thanks to you."

It hadn't been Hunter's fault that the papers had taken stories of his escapades and made him famous. Known as the Wolf of Haverstone, he was probably more of a target than anyone. Truly, he wouldn't be surprised if someone was trying to assassinate him this very minute, even though rumors of his retirement had hit the papers. It mattered not, for he was still a dangerous man, which is what made this mission seem odd. How was he to gain information when he hadn't the trust of anyone?

Suddenly uneasy, Hunter leaned back and exhaled. "What is it? What aren't you telling me?"

"We've secured you a partner."

"I work alone."

Wilkins shook his head. "Not this time."

"You force me to be disagreeable in having to repeat myself a second time, sir. I work alone. I always have."

"Without offending your obviously delicate sensibilities

about needing any sort of help, I assure you, you are working with a partner this time. You have no cover; therefore, you will be making sure this person does the job and gleans the information needed from our list of suspicious gentlemen."

Anger welled in Hunter's chest. He bit his lip and looked away, into the empty dust of the fireplace. "Who?"

"Red."

"Absolutely not." He jerked his head toward Wilkins and cursed. "No. A woman? Are you mad?"

"No, but perhaps I'm a bit tired and desperate." Wilkins smiled then, and Hunter noticed the dark circles under his eyes as well as the lines forming around his downturned mouth.

Hunter sighed and closed his eyes. Never had he worked with a partner, and surely not a woman. It wouldn't be a good match. How was he to be agreeable with the same woman he wanted to bed as well as fight every second of the day? "Has something happened that I need to be aware of?" Hopefully Wilkins would take the bait. There was only one reason that the Crown would be this desperate.

Wilkins gave him a sad look then cursed as he walked to the door, shut it, and locked it. As he walked back to his seat he explained. "There are only a handful of people who are familiar with what I am about to tell you." Wilkins took a shuddering breath and closed his eyes. "The ciphers are being cracked. Somehow the French have unlocked the code."

Hunter shifted uncomfortably as his mind went back to the night he and Gwen had met. Was that what the gentlemen in Belgium had been passing back and forth?

No, it had to have been something else, for the French were currently losing the war. Though to be honest, many Englishmen had been slowly losing their fortunes by idly twiddling their thumbs at White's rather than taking care of their own lands. In thought, he shook his head. Impossible. If they had broken the ciphers, it would be evident from the course of the war. If Napoleon knew the disposition of the Seventh Coalition's forces, he would not be in retreat. He'd turn with one of those lightning strokes for which he was known, and defeat this coalition the way he'd defeated the six that had preceded it.

"Impossible."

"Apparently not. There are three men who know the code. We have reason to suspect it is one of them."

"How are the ciphers taken to the front lines?"

"Sir Hollins writes the codes taught to him by his mentor. The cipher is then given to Viscount Redding. Every Tuesday at precisely four o'clock in the afternoon he takes a carriage ride down Rotten Row, where he meets with the Earl of Trehmont. They discuss the weather and if a certain phrase is exchanged, they shake hands and the code is given to Trehmont to post." Wilkins bit his protruding lower lip, another tell of the man's nervousness.

"And if the phrase is not exchanged?"

"Each man goes on his way, a sure indicator that a code does not need to be delivered. The process is flawless."

Hunter thought about this for a moment. "So one of these men is a traitor."

"A dangerous traitor, Haverstone. We've followed each of them for weeks and come up with nothing." Wilkins looked down. "The war is not yet over. Wellington is forcing Napoleon's Imperial forces to retreat, but the emperor remains dangerous and if he defeats Wellington, the war could drag on for another decade. France cannot afford to lose and we cannot afford to let them win. We need our people to be behind us, to believe us. If not, our fate will be the same as theirs. We both know what happens to single-minded people when they lose their leaders. They become like sheep, and are easily led astray. We are at a critical moment in our country's history.

You will enter into society with Red and eliminate the moles if necessary."

"And our only suspects are Trehmont, Redding, and Hollins?"

"All of those gentleman are of high priority, but their help in the War Office has been outstanding. Part of your mission will be dependent on entering into these men's lives without appearing too obvious."

Hunter cursed. "Is that all, then?"

Wilkins coughed and looked away. "There is one more person we are investigating; however, it is much more..." Wilkins paused. "Delicate. We need to be sure he or she is not able to communicate any more with Napoleon's elite."

"He or she?" Confused, Hunter leaned his full weight on his legs as he pushed forward out of his chair, closer to Wilkins.

"Your partner, Red. Though it was not our fault that she was with Napoleon as long as she was, she suffered tremendously under the pressure of the assignment. Although we have no reason to believe she changed sides, we are concerned that she may be tempted to. Too long on the field and all that."

Gwen? Surely not! Hunter laughed aloud. "A woman?"

"It is no laughing matter."

"A woman?" he repeated, and shook his head. What was the world coming to? A woman was not intelligent enough to pull something like this off. Yet his heart clenched at the thought. For he used to know a woman who was more intelligent than the ton combined, but she was no longer breathing. Her smile was gone as was her soul.

His heart twisted painfully in his chest.

"I refuse to believe it."

"Be that as it may. We need you to help stage a debut. We believe if we set her up in society that the chips may fall precisely as we like. Not only will she be the center of attention given her certain reputation, but the men who you are investigating are all single and in need of wives. It has been blatantly suggested that they begin their search. Gwen is very capable of making a man want her."

Everything suddenly made sense to Hunter as he looked into his old friend's tired eyes. "And if she is not truly a traitor?"

"Then she is the perfect bait for who is. Not only will she be serving her country in picking out the mole, but she will draw him out," Wilkins finished.

Hunter couldn't remember a time he'd felt the need to be loyal. Dominique had been his only friend, and now that he was married, Hunter felt quite like a fish on land, flopping around without proper hydration. Gwen, however, spoke to him in ways he'd thought long dead. Ways that quite honestly scared the devil out of him.

If she was a traitor, she needed to be brought to justice. Even if it made him sick to think of it.

And if she was innocent…

"When shall I begin?"

"Tonight. There is to be a special party hosted by Montmouth. Red, or as you know her, Lady Gwendolyn, will be making her debut this evening. It will be up to you to…" Wilkins looked to the ceiling and shook his head before meeting Hunter's gaze yet again. "It will be up to you to pay special attention to her. It is imperative that it look genuine."

If his lust was any more genuine, the girl would end up with her skirts tossed to the sky in but a few hours. "Am I to understand that you need me to flirt shamelessly with the woman?"

Wilkins shook his head. "I need you to make her desirable and in true rakish fashion, set yourself up as the name whispered upon young ladies' lips. It will distract the gentlemen from pursuing the other ladies, leaving them to pursue Red."

"My, my." Hunter laughed bitterly. "Is that all?"

"No." Wilkins rose from his seat. "If you have reason to believe she is dangerous, I need you to eliminate her from the equation."

"Eliminate her," Hunter repeated, sick to his stomach as he remembered Gwen's saucy smile.

"Kill her, Hunter." Wilkins never used Hunter's Christian name; it made the situation too personal, too real. "Eliminate your target. After all, you are an assassin and the best spy the Crown has. It is what you do, is it not?"

Hunter regained his composure and gave a stiff nod. "It is what I do best."

"Then we will meet again in a few weeks. My thanks." Wilkins held out his hand and shook Hunter's firmly. "Do say hello to your grandfather for me. Shame that he can no longer speak, for I fear he would be able to shed light on this situation for us."

Hunter paused with a grimace. The subject of his grandfather was not something he desired to pursue, even if his grandfather by marriage had been one of the best spies the country had ever seen. Not to mention one of the premier men next to Scovell, who worked with the codes.

"You will need to speak to him about the three men we are investigating, Haverstone. After all, before his recent accident, he was very much still involved with the dealings of the War Office as well as the codes."

Hunter grunted, then left the room before he said something he'd regret. He had not spoken to Lainhart in years, and he had no desire to start now.

Hunter refused to take the blame for his grandfather's bitterness. They were not blood related, for he had been Lucy's grandfather. The old man always did have something to complain about, whether it be his granddaughter marrying too young, or marrying a man who worked for the Crown.

Hunter smirked. The old man got his wish in the end. For the week after his wife's death, Hunter had attended one ball and ruined everything.

"The chess pieces have been placed very nicely, don't you think?" the gentleman asked as he took a long sip of whiskey. The London sky was darkening as if it were in tune with the plans that lay ahead. Plans that had taken over ten years to fulfill. Finally, riches would be his.

"Yes, though I find myself at a loss. Why set up the girl when she is clearly innocent? Isn't our goal to trap the Wolf?"

"Bait, my friend." The man chuckled. "Little Red will be our bait, and the very thing that will push him over the edge."

"How do you know?"

The man threw the glass to the floor and stomped over to his partner, sneering in his face as he noticed the man's lips tremble in fear. "Because this isn't the first time I've betrayed the Wolf, and I doubt it will be my last." He released his trembling partner and cursed. "Now, stop dallying. We have a war to win."

It began to rain, which fit quite perfectly into his already frustrated mood. Hunter slowly made his way down the stairs into the street. Once he was inside his carriage, he threw off his hat and leaned his head against the cold leather interior.

London was the same.

Everything was the same.

From the dreary pungent smell, to the constant gray

skies, it was as if the city was mocking him. How was he to do his job when it was difficult for him to put one foot in front of the other without becoming paralyzed with grief?

The carriage moved slowly, causing an agonizing thump to begin in Hunter's chest. He passed Lucy's favorite park, her parents' townhome, and finally they passed Gunther's.

Hunter hit the side of the door with as much force as he could, which was poor considering his ill state. With a loud curse, he threw the door open just in time to spew the contents of his stomach into the street.

And directly onto a pair of shiny Hoby boots.

"Drinking so early in the morning? That is not at all like you, old friend." Dominique Maksylov, royal prince of Russia and new Earl of Hariss, shook his head in amusement while kicking his boots against the street in dismay.

"Apologies." Hunter cleared his throat and prayed his friend of ten years wouldn't notice the exhaustion and worry etched across his brow.

"For drinking or for being unable to handle your drink?"

"Neither." Hunter smiled the first real smile that day. "I had only one drink, if you must know, Mother. I was merely sick from the carriage ride. Never could sit backwards."

"If it helps, keep your curtains closed, Hunter." Dominique put his hand on Hunter's shoulder, making him feel immediately worse. Why the devil did Dominique have to be so blasted sensitive to everything Hunter was feeling? Truly, God was giving him a taste of his own medicine. Was it only a few months ago that Hunter had involved himself in helping his old friend find happiness? A bit of calling the kettle black, he suspected, now that the roles were reversed.

His eyes quickly scanned Dominique. Gone was his beastly appearance. His hair was trimmed short, and his smile appeared permanent. Hunter clenched his teeth and tried to pull away from Dominique's heavy hand.

But he held firm.

"Stay with us."

No, the last thing he needed was to be reminded about how bitterly *un*happy he was. Staying the Season with Dominique and his beautiful wife sounded just as fun as banging his head against a rock. "No."

"Yes."

"No, blast it all. Dominique, I cannot stay with you! I'll stay at one of my homes. I do have means." He jerked away and scowled.

"So it is to be like that?"

"I do not know what you are referring to. You always were vague with your words."

Dominique threw his head back and laughed before returning his twinkling gaze to Hunter. "I won't take no for an answer."

"Well…" Hunter crossed his arms. "It seems we are at an impasse. Shall it be pistols at dawn, then?"

Dominique squinted. "It is that bad then, isn't it?"

"What is?"

His friend swallowed and looked away. "It is your first time back since the accident."

Accident? To say it had been an accident was nearly unbearable, for that meant it could have been prevented. Should have been prevented. Hunter felt the all-too-familiar sting behind his eyes, the lump in his throat, and the pain that came when one was trying to hold in a decade of tears. "It is."

"If shooting me will make you feel better, I'll allow it. Just be sure to explain to my wife upon my death that your pride got in the way of taking help from a friend when you needed it the most."

Hunter rolled his eyes. "You always were dramatic."

"Compared to your current state, I'm a Greek comedy. I'll expect your things later this afternoon." Dominique turned on his heel and left.

Hunter wasn't sure how long he stared at the street. His footman cleared his throat several times, people passed him by, some pointed, others whispered. But he ignored everything save the sound of his heart beating. *Thump, thump, thump.* It should be a comfort, to know one had a healthy beat in his chest, but all it did was remind him that while his was beating, hers was not.

CHAPTER THREE

Wolf—
It seems we are to be partners. I would rather drown myself in the river Thames, but alas my country needs me, especially since their most notorious spy is rumored to have lost his touch. Shall we meet later, or did you need more time to bathe and eat chocolate?
—Red

GWEN LOOKED DOWN AT the paper and grimaced. It was worse than she'd thought if Mrs. Peabody was already picking up on Hunter's notorious affairs. What had he done that was so terrible all those years ago? She read on as her sister continued to laugh about their conversation.

It seems, dear readers, that the Devil Duke and Lord Rawlings have officially lost their titles as the worst sort of rake the ton has ever seen. They can thank me later for my kind words. Gentlemen, I enjoy tea and chocolates; you may send any sort of gift to my publisher.
Now on to more important topics. How, you may ask, have two

such notorious rakes been dethroned? Well, let us just say that the man many a rake used to look up to, has returned with a vengeance, and he doesn't care a whit about what he says or does. It shouldn't come as a surprise; after all, nobody could forget the incident of 1806, which I refuse to acknowledge, given the circumstances surrounding it. One thing I will say, however; ladies, beware of the easy smile and devil-may-care demeanor. They lead to one thing, and it isn't matrimonial bliss. Beware, the Wolf has returned and he, dear readers, is on the prowl. —Mrs. Peabody's Society Papers

"You may cease laughing now," Gwen scolded her sister Rosalind as she took another sip of tea, throwing the gossip rag onto the chair in disgust.

"I just cannot help myself." She wiped a tear of mirth from under her eye and gave Gwen's hand a squeeze. "It is just too funny for words. Debut? You?"

"I am of age!" Gwen raised her voice and then cleared her throat. "Do you not think it is time for me to settle down and find a husband?"

Rosalind sobered and looked down at her lap. "I wish every sort of happiness for you, sister. It is just..." She bit her lip. Gwen waited. "Do you think it is too soon since...?"

Gwen rolled her eyes. "How many times do I need to reassure you? Absolutely nothing happened while I was on my own. I realize I'm not ruined in your eyes and that the rumors have been extremely painful to hear, but sister, I am ready."

"...To enter into the lion's den, hmm?" Montmouth strode into the room and kissed his wife briefly across the mouth before taking a seat. It wasn't at all odd for him to take tea with them; he was, after all, family. Not to mention he acted in the place of their deceased father while their mother was currently in Bedlam.

"It will be fine." Gwen was reassuring herself as much as

she was them. It would never be just fine. She knew she was a social pariah. The ton caught wind that she had gone after her sister, alone, in a traveling coach as well as aboard a ship, and she was considered a jezebel of the first order. To add pain to the entire situation, there wasn't a day that went by when she wasn't propositioned by some sort of gentleman to be his mistress.

"Lady Gwendolyn, I've always admired you from afar, and now that you are ruined…" The man would always pause here, as if to give sensual effect to his words as his hand traced her collarbone. "Do you not wish for some sort of male protection? Or companionship? I believe we will get along quite well together."

Just thinking on it made her angry.

The last man who had propositioned her, Sir Kirkland, had hobbled away holding himself and cursing all women to perdition. She'd been quickly escorted from that ball.

"Gwen." Montmouth exhaled. "Are you sure you wish to debut, tonight of all nights? Why not wait a year, wait until another scandal."

"Do you truly think people would ever forget about mine, Stefan?" She'd always addressed him as such, and considering he was the closest family she had other than her sisters, he didn't seem to mind, but one could never be sure with Stefan.

He closed his eyes as if in pain. Rosalind patted his arm. "I do not wish for you to do this."

Gwen gave them each a warm smile and leaned forward. "I will be fine. Through all of this I have seen that I am stronger than even I give myself credit for. I very much wish to be married. At least by debuting, we will put a stop to all the propositions for being someone's mistress."

"Doubt that." Stefan snorted, clenching his fist. "But if you wish it, I will allow it."

Gwen had expected her heart to stop beating in that

moment. The last thing she wanted was to debut and go to a ball where everyone would stare at her and wonder if she still held her virginity. The women would gossip, the men would openly stare, and she would count herself lucky if she could escape the evening without at least three attempts from young gentlemen to kiss her or pull her into a corner.

Add that to the already nervous sensation of seeing Hunter Wolfsbane, Lord Haverstone, and she was ready to scream. But if this was the only way to be sure her family and her country were safe, she would do it. One last mission, one last time to prove to herself and Hunter that she was above the gossip, above the stares. She was her own woman, a modern woman. And if she wanted to debut after such a scandalous winter, then that was what she was going to do.

A plan began forming in her head.

"I see this makes you happy, Gwen, and for that I am happy." Rosalind rose and kissed her on the cheek.

"Oh yes," Gwen answered, twirling a piece of hair between her fingers. "This makes me very happy." She smiled warmly and rose from her seat. "If you'll excuse me then, I just have some preparations to make before this evening's ball."

"If you need help..." Rosalind touched her arm. "Allow me?"

"Of course." Gwen left the salon, her slippers sliding quickly across the floor as she made her way up to her rooms.

Hunter gazed up at the mansion in front of him and sighed. Clearly things were bad when he was going to the Beast for some cheering up. Dominique had been the most depressing fellow to be around before his marriage, and now it seemed that he needed to cheer up Hunter. There was something so tragically wrong with the thought.

He needed to get ahold of himself.

With another soothing breath, he ran up the stairs and knocked on the front door.

The butler answered and lifted an eyebrow.

And because Hunter needed a bit of cheering up…

And because he was feeling slightly inebriated since he had taken a few strengthening drinks of brandy before making his way over to the Hariss residence…

He sneezed in the butler's face.

"Apologies!"

The butler cursed, which everyone knew could get the man sacked; must have been a good sneeze. Hunter grasped the lapel of the butler's stiff jacket and wiped his face.

"State your business and be gone…, sir." The butler stepped away.

"My business is not your business, George."

"It's Samuel."

"Nathanial, listen here." Hunter leaned in. "I'm having my trunks sent over, and I'll also need a room."

"The hotel is down the street."

"Daniel! Where is your sense of humor?"

Samuel's shoulders puffed up; his cheeks soon followed. Interesting fellow, but Dominique was never one to hire conventional butlers. Weren't they supposed to be seen and not heard?

"Sir, I must ask that you—"

"Hunter!" Isabelle ran down the stairs. Silly girl, clearly she hadn't learned the ways a lady should behave. Not that he would want her any other way. Blast, she absolutely glowed.

"My lady, it seems your current state agrees with you." He leaned down to kiss her cheek but was interrupted by Samuel clearing his throat.

"Don't you have somewhere to be?" Hunter asked.

Samuel turned red.

Isabelle swatted Hunter. "I am so sorry, Samuel. The Duke of Haverstone is an old friend, and will be staying with us for the Season."

Was it Hunter's imagination or did the butler just curse under his breath as he walked away?

"Cheeky fellow."

"He's Russian." Isabelle shrugged. "Now, come have tea with me and tell me all about your reason for spending a Season in London. We both know you'd rather get trampled by a horse than marry."

Hunter flinched at her words.

Isabelle paused and looked at him with curiosity. "I didn't mean anything offensive, Hunter. It's just that..." Her eyes watered. Blasted emotional woman.

"It is nothing. I was merely shocked you still possessed a sense of humor after living with Dominique for a few months."

"I missed you, too," Dominique said, bounding through the room looking healthy, virile, and extremely satisfied with himself. Curse the man. Maybe Hunter merely needed to find himself a mistress.

After all, it had been several months since his last encounter, and that one had scarred him to such an extent he hadn't had the courage to face a woman again. The lady in question had drugged him within an inch of his life and then proceeded to eat her dinner whilst on top of him. The thought gave him a shudder.

"Still feeling under the weather?" Dominique poured them both a glass of brandy. At this rate, Hunter would be foxed before the ball this evening.

"No, simply repulsed that Isabelle would find you charming enough to share your bed every night."

Isabelle smirked. "Believe me, he's—" Her face flamed red as she looked down at her hands, making Dominique laugh aloud.

Incredible. Hunter was now in his own version of Hell. Marital bliss surrounded him, and memories of his dead wife plagued even his waking dreams. He hadn't thought anything could possibly get worse.

"What are your plans for the Season?" Isabelle tried her best to engage him in conversation.

Unfortunately, his mind was working quite slowly; he blamed the brandy. So he blurted out, "I'm to find a wife."

Dominique began coughing wildly while Isabelle laughed.

"I was not jesting."

"Oh," they said in unison, causing a painful silence to blanket the room.

"It is a mission of sorts, so if you see me acting…"

"Strange?" Isabelle offered.

"Like an idiot?" Dominique felt the need to chime in.

"Yes." Hunter gritted his teeth. "All of the above, I guess. It is of the utmost importance that you do not deter me from my act. After all, it must be believable."

Dominique sat across from him. "Mind if I ask what part you shall be playing this Season? Perhaps the prince? Mayhap the devoted lover?" His friend grinned and leaned back, clearly enjoying himself.

"More predator than lover, I'm afraid. I'm to be myself."

Silence. Again.

Isabelle squinted. "So you're to play the fool?"

"You wound me!" Hunter grinned. "At least you truly do still have your sense of humor, Isabelle. And yes, if that is how you see me, that is what I will be."

Dominique hadn't spoken. Hunter waited.

"Am I to believe you're going to revert back to the incident of 1806?"

"Why the devil does everyone keep bringing that up?"

Hunter demanded suddenly, wanting to pace the room and yell at the same time. First Mrs. Peabody and now his best friend. "It was not such a big catastrophe."

"You went to the regent's annual end-of-Season ball with all of your clothes as well as your wits, and left naked, drunk, and with several women on your arms."

Hunter scoffed. "You exaggerate."

"They groped you."

Hunter shook his head and looked away in hopes to appear bored, when really he was deuced uncomfortable that Dominique would talk of such in front of his wife.

"In public."

Hunter sighed. "I was foxed."

"Believe me, nobody will forgive you that even if you were foxed. I believe you left town the next day."

"Forgive me," Isabelle interjected. "But is that to mean that tonight will be your first night in society since?"

"The incident," both Hunter and Dominique finished in unison.

Her mouth formed an O before she closed it and smirked to herself. "So you're to be playing the rake?"

"My dear." Hunter leaned forward and brushed her arm with his gloved hand. "I am a rake."

Dominique cleared his throat as Isabelle jerked back and giggled behind her hand. "I'm sorry, Hunter. I just don't see it. You've always been so…" She shrugged. "Happy."

Her admonition made his heart lurch. Of course he acted happy. It was the only way to convince himself he was. If he stopped jesting and making a fool of everyone around him, then the silence would kill him. He was convinced that if he even spent one day without finding humor, even if it meant hurting others, then grief would destroy him. He had come close today. So dangerously close while he was in his carriage.

He could not. No, he would not allow himself that same

weakness again. She was dead. It was his fault. He would burn in Hell, and he needed to pay for his sins by living through certain torture every day without her. By breathing when air was suddenly missing.

Shrugging, he gave her a seductive smile, the kind where he purposefully drew his lips across his teeth as his eyes boldly scanned her body and then in a husky voice he said, "My lady, was that a challenge?"

Dominique took a step between them "Do not encourage him, my dear, truly. I do not wish to see him talk you out of your gown."

"I am a married woman. I am in love! I would never! Hunter is my friend!" Her words came out at a rapid speed.

"My dear." Dominique chuckled. "I do love you, and I trust you, but Hunter is…" He glared at Hunter then looked softly back at his wife. "The very devil possesses that man, for I've never seen so many married woman fall at his feet. He truly is the best kind of hunter."

"But what does one do…" Hunter asked as he rose from his seat, "when the hunter is also the Wolf?" With a wink in their direction, he walked toward the doors. "I assume I'm in the red room. I'll just see to my things."

Hunter walked briskly out of the room and toward the stairs, but Samuel stopped him in his tracks. A grim expression passed across the old butler's face before he held the platter in the air in front of Hunter, nearly taking off his nose in the process. "Your grace, this message was delivered for you."

"I feel at home already." Hunter grinned and slapped the butler on the back quite forcefully, making the man stumble a bit on his feet before rolling his eyes and turning away.

There was no seal on the letter. Curious, he opened it. A grin spread across his face so widely, he was sure he would be sore in the morning. A simple letter should not affect him so, but there it was, irritatingly making him want to smirk and pat himself on the back.

It read, *I'll be wearing a red cape. Try not to make a complete fool out of yourself.* —Red

Yes, tonight was going to be a lovely night indeed. He decided to pen her something back.

"I will be wearing nothing at all. —The Wolf"

Laughing aloud, he scribbled quickly on the bottom of the note and passed it on to the butler. With great gusto, he gave a deep bow to the silly man and whistled on his way to his rooms. Maybe, just maybe it wouldn't be such a horrible mission after all.

"Who is that from, dear?" Rosalind asked as Gwen stuffed the correspondence into her pocket. "Why are you so flushed? Are you feeling ill? Is this about tonight?"

Gwen gritted her teeth. Ever since her sister's marriage, she had turned into something of a stand-in mother. Not that Gwen minded, but in times like these, she truly valued her privacy. "Nothing to be alarmed about. Merely an old friend wishing to inform me of his dress so we may match tonight."

"His?" Rosalind repeated. "Gwen, do you have a tender for a young gentleman?"

"He isn't young, he's old and quite flighty. In fact, I'm sure he's just one drink away from dying. Do not trouble yourself with such things." Gwen gave her sister a cheeky grin before dashing up the stairs to ready herself for the ball.

Once she was inside the safety of her room, she pulled the letter out and bit back a curse. How was she to deal with this man every day of the Season? If anything, it made her resolve to finish up the mission that much more implacable. She needed to be finished with Hunter. It was hard enough that his face plagued her thoughts, his scorching kiss still made her dizzy.

Taking a calming breath, she rang for her maid. It was time to become Red. The type of scandalous girl worthy of a debut. If ruin was what they wanted, then ruin they were going to get.

CHAPTER FOUR

Red—

Bathe? Eat chocolate? You naughty little minx. If I bring the chocolate, will you supply the bath? I promise to feed you. I don't, however, promise to be naked. I'll allow you the pleasure of disrobing me. Until we meet.

—The Wolf

GWEN WAS A WOMAN. Well, of course she was a woman, his body would never let him forget that little tidbit. Regardless, if she thought he wouldn't want to brief her before their meeting, she was sadly mistaken. He'd never worked with a partner before, and he wasn't about to allow her to ruin the mission by her inability to change her sex. He winced. Perhaps that was harsh. To change her sex meant...

With a curse, he rounded the corner where the servants' entrance was located and waited. It was the only location, Gwen had assured him, that would not be run down with people.

After ten minutes, he began walking back and forth on

the grass, or to be honest, stomping. The ball was to commence soon.

And she was late.

Women.

He huffed on a cheroot for five minutes and kicked some stones with his polished shoes. What the devil was taking her so long? One would think a spy, or at least a good spy, knew why it was important to be on time.

The cheroot suddenly went bitter in his mouth. He spit it out and cursed, running a hand through his hair. Would he always be haunted by his tardiness? Would everything serve to remind him of *her*?

"You're early," a feminine voice announced from the doorway.

"No." He turned. "You're l—" Not only was he instantly aroused but he suddenly could not remember what he was going to say. He felt his eyes widen as they strained to take in her dress. It was red. Not pastel, not white, but red. The very color only married women and those of ill repute chose to wear. Perhaps she could get away with it. If her hair wasn't so dark and her skin so pale. Her lips were painted just slightly, and he couldn't help but wonder if they tasted the same as before. Like fresh mint and warm berries.

He cleared his throat and regained his composure, but just by an inch. "You look beautiful."

"Well, thank you. I thought—"

"However," he interrupted, "you must change immediately."

"Pardon?"

"Did I speak too quietly? Perhaps I had a bit of a stutter? Or are you merely hard of hearing? Oh, I know!" He snapped his fingers and gave her a grin. "Were you so distracted by my appearance? Yes, I've had many a woman comment on that very thing. It's the eyes. I like to think of them as golden amber. You may refer to me as a god if you like. I won't mind." He stepped out of the shadows and peered down at her. "Regardless of how you address me, or your reason for not understanding, you still need to change."

"Absolutely not!" Gwen took a step back, but he snaked his arm around her and pulled her flush against his chest.

"I see you are going to be difficult." He smirked, quite enjoying the way her body felt in his arms. Curse the ball, he'd rather stay right where he was.

Her eyes narrowed as she pulled her head back so their foreheads wouldn't touch. "I'm not trying to be anything. I'm merely offended that you want me to change. I happen to like my gown."

"You and every other gentleman with a heartbeat. You cannot simply waltz into the ballroom dressed like a courtesan."

"But Hunter," she leaned in and whispered, so near his lips it was painful, "who said anything about waltzing?" In a flash, she maneuvered her way out of his hold and winked. "I plan on walking."

"Not like that." He pulled her arm again. This time she tried pinning him against the wall, but he beat her to the task, his legs straddling hers in a hold he was certain she wouldn't get out of. "Men will not take you seriously. You are supposed to be making a debut. You are husband-hunting, sweet." He ran his free hand down the side of her face. "And you look nothing like a dutiful wife."

"What do I look like?"

"A whore."

"Better a whore than a has-been."

Rage took over, pumping through his veins. "Did you just call me a has-been?"

"Did you just call me a whore?" she countered.

He loosened his hold on her, but her haughty eyebrow

chose that exact moment to lift, as if announcing to the world that she had bested him.

"Let me see." His lips came crushing down on hers. He forced his tongue into her mouth, shamelessly ran his hands down her naked arms. She pushed him back, her face a mixture of hurt and anger. "That is why you cannot wear that dress."

"Why?" Her lower lip quivered.

"Because, my dear, a whore would never respond like you did. It would be a dangerous game to play. And you, love, would not be the victor."

He brushed his lips against her cheek and began walking away.

"Hunter." Her voice was hoarse and angry. "What was so bad about my response?"

He froze in his steps and turned around. "I don't recall saying it was bad." With a smirk he walked away, clenching his fists as hard as he could so he would not be tempted to run back to her. That would put an immediate stop to his mission.

That dress. Lust screamed at him to do something about that dress. Blast it all! The woman was going to get herself killed! Men were not as feeble as she would like to believe. One look from her, in that dress, and a man would move mountains for one night with her. Unfortunately, because of her reputation, they would merely attempt to steal her away into the dark gardens. The thought made anger anew flush through his system. He wasn't sure what made him feel so protective of her. He'd never worked with a woman before. It wasn't as if he'd never seen a woman either! He'd had his share of… excursions. Granted, none of them had her breasts or lips, or smile, for that matter. But he had always thought it easy — a simple transaction and they parted ways.

With Gwen, he had this insane desire to protect her. Yet what if he was the one who needed protection? If she wasn't who she said she was, if her loyalty had been bought? It was a dangerous game they were playing.

One thing was for certain, he didn't need to make the girl desirable. After tonight, she'd have every available gentleman prostrate at her feet. The rub, it seemed, was how he was going to discover if she was a double agent. And if not, what influential person was no longer loyal to the Crown?

That went well. He waited in the shadows while the Wolf stomped off in the opposite direction of the girl. Red put her hands on her hips and scowled after him. Yes, his partner was very correct in his assumption. The woman would be quite a tasty morsel for the Wolf. He would feast upon her until he was weak, both physically and emotionally, and in the end, he would sacrifice his soul to keep her alive. Even if it meant treason.

Confusing, irritating, ridiculous man! *Who kisses like a god.* "Gwen!" she yelled at herself and closed her eyes, trying to focus on her mission, focus on her one goal for the night. But all she could think about was his lips against hers. She hated that the minute he kissed her, she was lost. Her knees had gone weak, her breath had mingled so tightly with his that she wasn't sure if she was even breathing anymore. His touch made her shiver. The very reason she had for working with the man seemed to dissipate. She thought in vain that, if she were merely reminded of his rakish ways and ridiculous smile, her heart and mind would immediately reject him. He would be a poison to her. Never faithful, never kind, always teasing. Besides, there was something about his eyes, some hidden secret, or perhaps it was an agenda. Or maybe he really was just, plainly, a wolf. A predator.

How was she to ever experience happiness if she had to compare Hunter's kisses with others? Unfortunately, he knew just how desirable he was. Which meant she had to work that much harder to keep him away if she wanted to escape the Season unscathed.

She looked down at her dress and sighed. Blast the man, he was right. Though she would never admit it to him, she'd known it was a bad idea from the start, but her nerves and determination had gotten hold. Her pride no longer existed. It had disappeared the day she arrived back in London, only to find her name scattered about Mrs. Peabody's society papers.

Things had become progressively worse when she'd gone to a small gathering only to find herself being whispered about and ignored. A few even gave her the cut direct. She was labeled as used goods. Never mind that she had only ever kissed one man. But that one kiss might as well have ruined her, for ever since that day, she hadn't felt the same.

Cursing Hunter for a good five minutes, using as many languages as she could think of, she finally ran back through the servants' entrance and up to her rooms.

"The white one," she directed to her maid. "I've decided to change into the white gown and I will wear the red hooded shawl as planned."

"As you wish." Her maid gave her an odd look but made quick work of undressing her. The red gown had been daring in color, but the white gown was daring in a completely different way. For starters it was dangerously low, even for a married woman to be wearing. The bodice had pearls sewn into the material and a very tiny slit went up to her knee underneath the first layer, making it possible if one looked very hard to see part of her leg.

It was all part of her plan. Look daring, be daring, and

gain secrets. After all, the only way she could imagine gaining an offer and learning information about those disloyal to the Crown was to have gentlemen find interest in her.

Before tonight, she could have had the best personality in the world and they would only offer her companionship.

After tonight, she was planning on unleashing everything she had. Hoping, desperately that it would work.

Hunter waited a half hour before going through the front entrance. He pulled a flask out of his pocket, ran a hand roughly through his hair, and loosened his cravat, just slightly.

All in all, he hoped his appearance looked as if he had just finished having the best night of his life and eagerly sought more companionship. Not the type of entrance he had hoped to make upon returning to London. But then again, he hadn't wanted to return. Ever.

When he was announced the room went silent.

He always did like being the center of attention; at least then he could ignore that irritating pain in his heart that told him he was alone.

"I don't believe I've ever had such a warm welcome. You are, of course, allowed to applaud as you see fit." He winked in Montmouth's direction. The duke narrowed his eyes; his wife, however, looked quite amused as she began clapping wildly.

The rest followed suit, most likely trying to figure out why the devil they were clapping for a man they'd rather see hanging by a noose, especially considering how much he offended their delicate sensibilities.

He gave a little bow to his audience, and immediately went to Montmouth's side. "A pleasure, as always, your grace."

"Doing it a little brown, aren't we, Haverstone?"

"Whatever do you mean?" Hunter tilted his head and boldly eyed the Duchess of Montmouth. "I was merely trying to remedy an awkward situation."

"You did lovely." The duchess reached out to him.

He grasped her hands and pulled her close. "Do you really think so?"

She gasped as Montmouth pried her hands away from Hunter's grasp.

The duke cursed but a small smile danced across his lips. "I think I speak for every married man here: find yourself a woman and settle down before you find yourself fighting in a duel."

"But your grace…" Hunter tried to look horrified. "Those are illegal! I am, after all, a lover, not a fighter."

The duchess burst out laughing as Hunter was ushered away by Montmouth at alarming speed.

"Must you always be so—"

"Charming? Dashing?" Hunter filled in, suddenly enjoying himself now that the pain in his heart had begun to slightly fade.

"I was going to say irritating," Montmouth ground out as he reached for a glass of champagne. "Just be careful not to seduce any women who are married and you will do just fine."

"Why, Monmouth! Are you of all people giving me sane advice? Is it because you care for my welfare? Must admit, my tastes haven't ever swung in that direction, you silly man, but I thank you for your concern."

"I do not care a whit for you."

"Surprising." Hunter gulped the rest of his wine and placed the empty glass on a passing tray, then grabbed another. "And here I thought we were to be going shooting and riding tomorrow, all the while laughing into the sunset.

I'm so disappointed."

"Clearly." Montmouth grunted. "Just be careful. This is the duchess's first ball of the Season and she is nervous."

"Then perhaps her husband should go about easing her nerves." Hunter grinned wolfishly, and when Montmouth made no move in her direction, Hunter added, "Or perhaps her tastes are running more on the wild side tonight, hmm?"

Montmouth's arm shot out to stop Hunter. "One week."

"Pardon?" Hunter shrugged out of the duke's hold.

Montmouth slapped him forcefully on the back. "One week before you fight your first duel."

"Are we taking bets then?" Dominique walked up and grinned.

"Absolutely." Montmouth shook Dominique's hand while Hunter rolled his eyes and ignored their bidding. "Shall we put it in the books at White's?"

Hunter snorted and gave them both bored looks. "May as well line your pockets at my expense, though it saddens me to tell you nobody will challenge me to a duel."

Dominique cursed. "He's right."

"Why the devil not?" Montmouth seemed terribly disappointed that Hunter would go on living another day.

"Because they would lose." Hunter shrugged, his eyes still trained on the staircase where Gwen was to be descending. Where the blazes was she?

"How can you be so certain?" Montmouth really wasn't letting this go. Perhaps when this was all over with Hunter could fake his own death so the duke could sleep peacefully at night.

"Is that your way of asking for a demonstration?" Hunter's voice was light but his glare was penetrating.

Montmouth took a step back, his eyes never leaving Hunter's. "There is something wrong with you."

At that, Hunter threw his head back and laughed bitterly.

"Believe me, I know."

The hair on the back of his neck stood at attention. She was here, but where the blazes was she? He ran a shaky hand through his hair and exhaled. The smell of rose water filled the air. His breath caught, as he clenched his fists and felt a hand on his shoulder.

"Surprise," a sultry voice said behind him. For a minute he felt his mask, his façade fade away as he entertained the thought of being with her, and only her at the ball.

If things were different. If she truly were looking for a husband, would she dare look in his direction?

"Lady Gwendolyn." Hunter turned around with every intention of giving her a curt bow and asking for a dance.

Good intentions died the minute he set eyes on her person.

"I thought I told you to change?"

"Yes, well, as you so lovingly pointed out, I'm hard of hearing. Besides, I still listened."

"Yes, if listening means going behind my back and doing something just as scandalous."

"It's a cape."

"It's red."

"My, my, my, what very big eyes you have to notice such a bright color, Wolf."

Hunter gripped her elbow and pulled her toward the dance floor, shouting to Montmouth, "Permission to waltz with the fair lady?"

"Absolutely not!" Montmouth ground out.

Dominique elbowed him. Montmouth cursed and finally gave a nod.

"Lovely." Hunter placed his hands on Gwendolyn's body, nearly swearing as he did so. "I have half a mind to punish you."

Gwen glared. "And I have half a mind to slap you across

the face."

"Pray tell, what is stopping you?" Hunter crooned into her ear.

"I do not wish to touch you."

"Have you taken to lying now that you're a spy?"

Gwen tensed in his arms. "Are you that confident in your looks, your grace?"

"Not at all," Hunter answered honestly, pulling her closer than what was considered appropriate. "I was speaking of my skills in the bedroom, of course."

"I wouldn't know."

Hunter chuckled warmly, his lips nearly touching her ear. "Would you like to?"

Gwen jerked back, her face flushed. "You're making a fool of yourself."

"As are you." He assessed her coldly; she squirmed in his arms. "The way I see it, every person in this room is straining to hear our conversation. Alas, we are speaking in hushed tones, so they cannot know what we speak of. But care to guess what they do know?"

"Not really." She clenched her teeth. "But I'm sure you'll tell me anyway."

"Good girl." Hunter chuckled and pulled her body more tightly to his. "At this very moment, the ladies are commenting on your blush, the way it covers your cheeks and dips ever so naughtily down your neck into the deep canvas of your breasts." Hunter hoped what he was doing would work, because if it didn't, he was going to have to excuse himself and jump into the Thames in order to cool his arousal.

Gwen gasped.

"The men, however, are another matter entirely. You see, men notice the blush; that much is true. It tells them that against popular gossip, you are in fact quite innocent. And the way your eyes blaze tells them the rest."

"My eyes?"

"Yes."

The dance was nearing an end. Hunter guided their steps to where she would be most visible by the ton.

"I don't understand. What do my eyes have to do with anything?"

"They show your spirit. Your fire, but my dear, they speak one language I fear every man in this room is just begging to use with you."

She lifted an eyebrow.

He leaned in, gripping her body so she could not run off, and whispered into her ear. "Sex. You look like sex."

Gwen jerked away from him, nearly tumbling to her bottom, righted her skirts, and slapped him across the face.

People gasped.

Women began to gossip, and as expected, a few women, ones he was sure had just given the girl the cut direct not a week before, were huddling around her and telling her to stay away from his evils.

Hunter rubbed his cheek and walked by a few gentlemen.

One stopped him. "I say, what did you do to make the lady so offended?"

"The lady did not care for my advances," Hunter admitted, appearing to look quite put out as he shook his head and cursed. "I thought she was tainted, but it appears the joke has been on all us young men. To think, she wants to marry! And it has been proven, though you did not hear this from me, that the lady herself is untouched."

"Untouched," another man whispered.

And much like wildfire, or a storm, or perhaps a giant explosion taking place in the room, it was spread that Gwen was entering into the marriage mart, and she was completely pure.

Hunter walked off to a darkened corner and exhaled.

"Well done," Wilkins said behind him.

Hunter did not turn around; instead he nodded his head just once and went in search of Gwen. By now she would be exhausted, and he needed to watch her every move. The game had been laid out, the pieces moved.

CHAPTER FIVE

Wolf—
The only thing you'll be eating is your words and perhaps any crumbs of humility I decide to throw your way! You are a deceitful, horrible person! If I find myself in your arms again before the week is out I will pull a pistol on your most useful and favorite anatomical part!

—Red

THE MAN WAS EITHER a genius or purely insane. Men came in throngs from the ballroom's distant corners, each of them expressing sudden interest in taking her for a ride in the park or asking her opinion about some new poetry written by Byron. Another asked her if she was free to marry as soon as the end of the week!

At least now she was able to concentrate on her targets.

Wilkins had sent her a note stating that the following three men were suspected of treason.

Lord Trehmont, Sir Hollins, and Lord Redding.

Men who, by all appearances, valued propriety above all

else.

But she knew their secrets.

Trehmont was in debt up to his ears, and to some powerful people within the fallen French aristocracy. Meaning they were finally calling out all the debt. But was he desperate enough to betray his country? Or murder someone because of it?

Hollins was a young idiot who had more money than sense. His desire was to buy himself a better title, but nobody seemed to be willing to give him the time of day. It was rumored he also enjoyed sexual escapades that were enough to make any debutante, or woman for that matter, cringe. She could see him killing someone; in fact, she could see him doing a lot of terrible things in order to gain power.

And finally Redding. Unfortunately, she knew nothing about him. Only that he was devastatingly handsome and rumored to have grotesque scars from the war. Though one couldn't see the scars by looking at him.

He still walked with a slight limp, but that didn't keep females from chasing after him. The poor man often resorted to hiding; he was akin to the last antelope at a dinner party for lions.

With a sigh, Gwen squared her shoulders and batted her lashes at the men surrounding her, each of them in her mind a suspect.

She ignored most of the conversation, allowing them to fuss about her and compliment her dress. The smile felt frozen across her face as each and every one of the men, around ten of them, continued to pay her false compliments, all the while leering at her breasts and panting after her.

Gwen wasn't vain enough to think it was her looks that gained her acceptance, but the fact that the great Wolf had declared her pure and she had slapped away his advances. Men.

After being asked if she was receiving callers in the afternoon, to which she replied yes, she decided to remove herself from the situation.

"Gentlemen, it is dreadfully hot, is it not?" With a flourish, she pulled out her fan and began dramatically fanning her face.

"Well then." Trehmont cleared his throat and stood directly in front of her. "It seems all the lady needs is a brisk walk into the cool night air with a willing gentleman." He reached for her free hand, but was slapped away by another intruder.

"Terribly sorry, Trehmont, but it seems the lady has already promised to take the air with me." Hunter's voice was like silk compared to the rest of the men's.

"As the lady wishes." Trehmont grimaced, showing his vast irritation. Gwen thought it a kindness that she would talk to him at all, considering the circumstances. It would be a trial to even speak with the man longer than a few minutes, let alone let him touch her person.

She shivered at the thought as Hunter led her toward the outskirts of the ballroom.

"Trembling beneath my touch, my sweet?"

Gwen rolled her eyes but kept her smile firmly in place as they passed curious onlookers. "Yes, it seems you've caught me, Hunter. Your touch turns me to liquid, your kiss makes my knees weak, please, let us marry and be done with this whole charade."

Hunter sighed. "I leave you for five minutes and the dove turns into a shrew."

"Are you always this poetic?"

Hunter clenched her arm tighter as he led her toward the doors to the balcony. "Always."

Gwen smirked and stole a sideways glance at the man. His golden eyes were trained on the door, his perfect devil-may-care smile in place, but he was rigid with tension.

She cleared her throat. "You should have given me more time with the gentlemen. I need to be in their confidence if I am to find out their secrets."

Hunter snorted and finally looked at her. "Believe me, they were within seconds of blurting every blasted secret in the known universe." Why did he sound so irritated?

"You need to let me do my job."

He smirked. "And you, my dear, need to allow me to do mine." He pushed through the door and led her out into the cool night air. "Besides, it is our job to leave them a little trail of bread crumbs." His eyes gazed at her face and then lower. "Very attractive little crumbs."

"Bread crumbs?" Gwen repeated, ignoring the shiver his look gave her. He was her partner. Perhaps if she kept chanting that over and over again, she would forget his kiss. And the way his golden eyes caressed her skin.

"Why, yes." Hunter released her arm and pulled out a cheroot. "Give a squirrel a basket full of nuts and it will gorge itself or worse yet, covet the nuts and no longer search for more."

"Nuts? Now you're comparing men to nuts?"

Hunter scoffed as he took a long draw of the cheroot. "Absolutely not. I'm comparing men to squirrels."

"Oh."

"You, my dear, are the nut."

"Oh?" Gwen had to clench her hands behind her back to keep from lunging after the man.

"Why, yes." Hunter blew out another puff of smoke and grinned. Blast, how she hated that grin. She looked away as he continued to speak, his chest puffed out much like a peacock when mating. "When men or animals, for that matter, are in pursuit, they are easily bored and distracted. We need to make this game a challenge."

RACHEL VAN DYKEN

"So now I'm part of a game." Gwen looked up at Hunter just as he threw down his cheroot and turned his full male arrogance upon her. Shocking that God didn't feel the need to strike the man down for his petulance.

"All women are. I'm just making it more interesting for the male sex, and easier on you."

Gwen pasted a sweet smile on her face and walked toward Hunter, stopping when she was inches away from his devilishly handsome lips. "So, is it my sex that causes you to offer this extra help? Or your kind heart?"

"Your sex." He nodded.

"Because you have no heart," she concluded.

"There's that." He leaned in and sniffed her hair. Why the devil was he sniffing her? "But there is also the distinct truth about women that men find impossible to resist."

"And what's that?" Gwen breathed in the scent of his breath, a mixture of port and smoke, so alluring she almost closed her eyes.

"The chase, my dear. All men, all animals, all hunters need the chase. And sweetheart, we are in the hunt of our lives."

"And you?" she challenged, placing a hand on his firm shoulder. "Your very name assumes the title hunter."

He swallowed and took a step back as her arm fell to her side. "Never mistake me for the hunter, when I very well could be the wolf." He nodded and offered his arm. "That is the first rule of spying, Gwen. We are all wolves in sheep's clothing; every last one of us could be guilty of treason. It is our job to find the wolves without killing the sheep."

His eyes pierced hers, looking directly through her almost as if he suspected her of being a wolf. Which was utterly ridiculous.

The gravity of the situation rested quite heavily on her shoulders as she whispered, "And what if we kill some sheep in the process?"

"If you're as good as you say you are, Red, that won't happen."

CHAPTER SIX

Red—

How is it that you are familiar with... how did you word it? Oh yes, my favorite anatomical part. Pray tell, are we discussing my hands?

—Wolf

GWEN STUDIED HUNTER'S FACE. A heaviness seemed to descend upon him. "Have you lost many sheep?"

Hunter swallowed and looked down. "Some."

"I'm sorry." Gwen reached out to touch his arm, but he jerked away and laughed.

"Don't be. It is all part of the work we do. Besides, sheep are stupid. They are among God's silliest creatures." Hunter gave her a silly grin and shrugged. "Perhaps it is why we are compared to them in the Bible. All sheep go astray."

Gwen opened her mouth to speak but was interrupted by a male voice.

"I was wondering when you would make your sorry presence known."

Hunter rolled his eyes and turned to the man. "Lord Eastbrook, how lovely to see you after all these years."

"Nine." The man pointed at Hunter. "Nine blasted years, friend."

"Do not call me friend," Hunter snapped.

Eastbrook shook his head. "What has happened to you? Do you not realize you have a responsibility to this family?"

Hunter rolled his eyes. "Spare me the lecture, cousin. It's my business and mine alone why I've returned."

"He wants to see you. He has something for you."

Hunter cursed fluently and leaned over the balcony. Gwen wasn't sure if she should leave or stand there like a fool.

"Eastbrook." The man stepped out of the shadows and held out his hand to her. "I know it isn't at all proper to introduce myself without proper introductions being made. I know your brother-in-law quite well."

"And that makes you harmless?" Gwen lifted an eyebrow in question.

Eastbrook smirked. "Absolutely not. Forgive the intrusion." His golden hair shimmered in the moonlight. He truly was quite handsome, but looked nothing like Hunter. "Tomorrow, cousin. He would like to see you tomorrow."

With one final glance at Gwen, Eastbrook gave a quick bow, meeting her gaze for a brief second and then he turned on his heel and left.

"Well, it's been an eventful evening. I do hope I'm not ruined for standing out on the balcony with two devilishly handsome men," Gwen lamented, trying to pull Hunter from his paralyzed state as his body seemed to be frozen in one spot.

"He is not handsome."

Gwen laughed. "After all that was said, you choose that particular sentiment to respond to? I didn't know you had a cousin."

RACHEL VAN DYKEN

"I don't."

"But…"

"I'm no longer recognized by that side of the family."

"But surely there is a mistake! They are your family, blood related and—"

Hunter shook his head. "Not blood related. My family line was snuffed out the minute my father and brother died. Eastbrook is my cousin by marriage."

Gwen felt her stomach drop to her slippers. "You rogue! You're married!"

Hunter chose that moment to turn around and glare. "Not that it's any of your business, but no I'm no longer married."

"So you are divorced."

Hunter cursed. "This conversation is finished." Cursing, he pulled her flush against his body and kissed her lips. The kiss was forceful and aggressive, then he pulled a tendril of hair from her coiffure allowing it to fall to her shoulders. "There. Now return to the ball."

"But I look like I've been out here having an assignation with a man."

"Precisely," Hunter said in clipped, even tones. "But only a man will notice the look of a woman in a lust-filled haze. And the type of men you need to attract will want to sample some of your goods."

"Lovely," Gwen said dryly.

"Play nice, sweetheart." Hunter winked and patted her bottom as he slipped past her. The absolute devil! She lunged for him but he was already down the stairs to the balcony, leaving her no choice but to sneak back into the ball. Looking and feeling very much like a whore. Some debut.

CHAPTER SEVEN

Red—

If you murder me in my sleep, does that mean we shall be sharing a bed? Imagine my surprise that you would be so forthcoming with your feelings. My dreams await you, sweet.
—Wolf

HUNTER WATCHED AS GWEN entered back into the ballroom. He'd had enough family dramatics to last him a lifetime tonight. The last thing he wanted to do was go visit Lucy's grandfather and allow him to lecture Hunter about why her death was on his head. He'd probably blame Hunter for the fact that someone was deciphering the codes for the French as well.

He reached for the flask of brandy in his jacket and took a few swallows. The night was eerily quiet. He took a few soothing breaths and leaned against the stone wall.

No doubt Gwen was inside, blushing to the roots of her hair. He hadn't meant to kiss her. Well, actually that wasn't entirely true. He'd meant to kiss her, just not so forcefully, nor did he mean for his tongue to accidently slip past the barrier between her lips and into the honey of her mouth. It also wasn't planned that his body would flare to life in such an embarrassing way that he could think of doing nothing except lifting her skirts against the wall and having his way with her.

He really did need to find a female companion, especially when difficult shrews who could be French spies were making him aroused.

The music trickled out of the ballroom. He hated balls. What was the point of women and men dancing around when the end was still the same? Marriage? Death? Sex?

Why not just skip the dancing and go straight to sex?

Why not skip the marriage and save yourself from impending depression.

He took another swig of brandy and groaned.

Clearly, he was getting too old for this. He wanted to go home and drown his sorrows in whiskey. He wanted to sit by the fire and pout. Female companionship, again, he needed it desperately.

Laughter echoed into the night air.

"But Viscount Redding, it isn't proper for us to be alone! And so soon after meeting!" Gwen giggled.

Hunter rolled his eyes. Any idiot could see Gwen was not prone to giggling. It was blasted irritating, seeing Redding put a hand across Gwen's arm as if she was his possession.

She belonged to no one.

Not even to Hunter.

He ignored the slight pain in his chest; must be too much drinking out in the cold. Even though his eyes begged him to look away as Redding caressed Gwen's face. He stayed trained on the man, ready to pounce at any moment.

"But my lady, you said you had something important to discuss with me. How could I, in good nature, allow us to have such a discussion with such impressionable people around?"

Hunter perked up. Something sounded wrong. What the devil was Gwen doing? He peeked around the corner. Gwen was grinning wildly at Redding, making Hunter want to rip the man's throat out.

Obviously that was the brandy speaking.

Not his need to have her.

Or his desire to bed her.

His breath quickened when she lightly touched Redding's arm. "They say you are a man of great secrets."

Redding pulled her flush against him. "And who are they, my dear?"

Gwen leaned in and whispered in his ear. Hunter strained to hear. Cursing, he listened for something — anything.

But soon Gwen's laughter filled the air as Redding kissed her hand and announced his departure. "I will think on these things, my dear, and thank you for your information. I find it enchanting." He kissed her hand and walked away, a stupid grin that Hunter wanted to destroy all over his face.

Gwen's smile fell. She pulled something out of her reticule and dropped it onto the ground and then briskly walked toward the side of the house where Hunter was standing.

She was up to something.

Spy or no spy. Partner or no partner. If he was to find the mole, he needed to snuff out the suspects. Starting with Gwen. He only hoped she would forgive him for what he had to do.

Gwen had done several things in her lifetime that she found disgusting. Flirting with a man should have been easy, but when that particular man sneered at her all the while leering at her breasts — she wanted to do nothing more than kick him in the shin, or perhaps his favorite anatomical part? Yes, her fingers itched for her knife.

She'd only meant to lure him away from the crowds of people in order to solidify his interest. If she was to be done with this mission, she needed to make sure the men put forth an effort to court her, and she would get absolutely nowhere with Hunter constantly interfering! Goodness. It was her job to help find the mole. But it was getting increasingly difficult as she realized that she knew nothing. Redding seemed innocent enough, and didn't seem the type to betray his country for money he clearly did not need. But Trehmont seemed to lack the backbone.

Her gaze flickered to the wall where she saw Hunter attempting to hide. The fool, did he not trust her to do her job? She pulled a note out of her reticule and let it fall to the ground. It said something akin to: "Touch me again and I'll murder you in your sleep."

Which would truly be a nice little love note for Hunter to read, suspicious man that he was. She had meant to send it the following day, but now was as good a time as any to make open threats. Especially considering he was spying on her rather than doing his job.

Did he expect her to do everything while he patiently flirted and watched from the sidelines?

With a sigh, she walked back toward the house. Hunter had apparently disappeared, which was fine by her. She was getting tired, and hadn't the energy to fight his wit or his charm.

She stumbled toward the front of the house and yawned when a loud crunch was heard behind her and then something struck her head. She fought to keep her eyes open, but failed as she succumbed to the darkness.

CHAPTER EIGHT

Wolf—

To visit you in a dream would be my worst nightmare. In fact, as I write this very note, I find myself shaking with fear. Not because I am afraid of the big bad Wolf, no, of course not. It is because in your dreams you deem what is appropriate and naturally I have certain morals against walking around naked with a salivating wolf gazing upon me, ready to eat my flesh. Hope you understand. Perhaps the woman from the inn is still available. After all, she did feed you, and we both know how much wolves like meat.

—Red

"IT SEEMS THE WOLF has taken Red captive," the man announced, rubbing his eyes with the back of his hand. It had been a long night. To make matters worse, the Wolf was going to get all the answers he needed within the next few hours, throwing quite a hitch in their plans.

His partner laughed. "Why, that is more perfect that I could have planned it!"

He stared at the man he'd called friend for the past ten

years and cursed. "What do you mean? He will discover her innocence!"

"He will torture her in order to obtain it, then spend the rest of his days feeling like the guilty sod he is. He'll lick her wounds for her, he'll pant after her, and again, I say, it is more perfect than we could have planned."

He chose to say nothing.

"Have you the codes?"

He walked forward and slid them across the table. "The new codes, as you asked. Will you be planting them this week?"

A long pause and then, "No, the time is not yet right. We must wait until every player is either engaged or eliminated."

"And who will be doing the eliminating?"

"Why, me, of course. After all, I failed so many years ago. I will not fail again."

Hunter felt like an absolute cad. Ten years. Ten years of being a spy and torturing people for information, and his blasted hands still shook as he tied the ropes firmly around Gwen's hands.

He hadn't any choice. That was what he kept telling himself as he gagged her and put the blindfold on. That was what he said to himself when he lit the fire and put her chair dangerously close to it.

And that was what he told himself when he returned to his abandoned house, the same house he had shared with Lucy, only to find it dusty and hollow.

Gwen had no idea this ghost of a house existed, nor that it was his. It would be the perfect hideaway until their little visit was complete.

One thing was for certain; when she woke up, she was

going to be furious. But he had to test her loyalty. Not just for him, but for the protection of her family and Montmouth, even though the man clearly hated him. If Gwen, a part of their family, truly was a French loyalist, then they were all in grave danger.

"Wake up," he snapped, kicking the chair.

Gwen moaned, her head dropped, and then she jerked back and yelled, "Where am I?" Astonishing that she could form the words against the gag; perhaps he had tied it too loosely?

"Does it really matter? After all, you are tied to a chair."

"Get this off." Her head jerked from side to side. Amazing, how silky her hair was up close. His obsession was bordering on insanity.

"That I cannot do." He purposefully spoke in perfect French to keep her from guessing his identity.

"Why?"

"You have something I want." He rolled his eyes at his choice of words, and then fought the urge to curse himself as he watched her bosom rise and fall with exertion. And then an entirely new plan formed in his mind.

Torture. For both of them most likely, but torture nonetheless. This way he wouldn't have to scar that perfect skin, or worry about truly frightening her.

He just wasn't sure if he could do it without exploding on the spot.

"My love," he purred, as his voice dropped into a seductive whisper. "You are such a fine, fine beauty." He gently pulled the gag down so she could speak. His gaze lingering on her lips like a man starved.

"I'm rolling my eyes right now, but you can't see me," Gwen said boldly.

Minx. "I would love to see your eyes but then you would know my identity and we cannot have that, my beauty." He was laying it on thick and arousing himself in the process. Who was seducing whom?

"Of course we can't," Gwen agreed. "Then it wouldn't be nearly as fun, hunting you down and killing you."

"Are you a good hunter?"

"The best."

"Hmm." Hunter stood behind her, his hands on her creamy shoulders, then with slow movements, he slid his hands down roaming her chest. "I highly doubt that, my sweet."

She froze under his touch, and then the witch actually relaxed and leaned her head against his arm. "That feels good."

I know. Believe me, I know. He dipped his hands further into the top of her dress and tugged it down.

"Is your plan to seduce me?" Gwen asked. Hunter was so distracted by her creamy white skin he almost didn't hear her question.

"But of course. Love always comes before war, does it not?" He kissed the top of her head. "And I plan on loving you several times before the evening is done."

"And then?"

"I kill you."

"Oh." Gwen shrugged. "At least I'll be loved before I die."

Frustrated that she wasn't responding, Hunter growled and kicked the bottom of the chair, making it skitter closer to the fire.

She smiled. "A pitiful kick. Are Frenchmen not stronger than that?"

Hunter hated himself in that moment. Hated that he was doing this to her, but it was a means to an end. Cursing, he kissed her and bit her bottom lip, hard enough to draw blood. Immediately regretting the action, he jerked back.

"More animal than man, it seems," Gwen noted as her tongue reached out to lick the blood from her bottom lip.

"You have no idea." Hunter swore. Angry at himself that he was aroused the whole time he was causing her emotional distress, but it wasn't what he was doing, it was her cool indifference, her reactions to what he was doing, that made his blood boil with lust. Blast, but she was strong.

Terror did not even begin to describe what Gwen was feeling. She'd never been tortured, or captured for that matter. Oh, men had put their hands on her, thinking her nothing but a French whore, for that had been one of her many identities, though she hadn't shared that little piece of information with anyone. It wasn't as if she had slept with any man, but it had been a close call. But her current predicament was spiraling out of control. If she escaped, it would not be without losing something important to her. The only thing she had left of any worth. Her virginity.

But something about the man's kiss was familiar. Enough to make her hate herself for enjoying the pleasure of his lips upon hers. Obviously, she was losing her mind and going just as mad as Hunter, for even though she had a blindfold across her face, she almost thought it was he and not some mad Frenchman.

The man paced in front of her, cursing in French.

"Well," Gwen sighed. "Get on with it then."

"With pleasure." He straddled her lap and kissed her firmly across the mouth. His kiss was her end. It had to be. For no man had ever kissed her in such a way, with such raw passion, such desire. His tongue pushed into her mouth, forceful and aggressive. He tasted so sweet. His warm hands cupped her cheeks and then moved lower down her shoulders. Every single caress was like a fire being lit inside her. But, to be fair, she was also dangerously close to the flames; she could feel the heat licking at her slippers. The passion mixed with heat was a painful yet arousing situation.

The man moaned into her mouth. She briefly contemplated kicking him but it would do nothing except arouse him more, considering he was straddling her. Perhaps this was his torture, and what a magnificent torture it was.

Gwen's lips parted; a small cry escaped them as her head fell back. "More," she said. "Give me more." Although it was no pretense, she hoped that he would at least untie her hands so that she could wrap them around his neck, and in that moment she would escape. She would flee, even if his kiss was the very devil.

"First, tell me what I want to know." A large smooth hand reached underneath her skirts, trailing up her calf to the ties of her satin stockings.

"What would you like to know?" She swallowed the bile in her throat. Was he going to rape her?

"Who do you work for?"

"Myself." She grinned, though she became more ill by the minute.

"And the French?"

"Are no longer a threat," she answered boldly. Why would he ask about his own people?

"Oh?"

Gwen nodded and squirmed beneath him, making it absolute torture to be in that position and do nothing about it. "I'm loyal to my country."

Hunter leaned forward and kissed her again. "Even in the midst of absolute torture, you would still stay loyal to your country?"

"Yes."

"So we skip to the main course." Hunter pulled away from her lap and went to the table to grab his knife. He also needed time to cool his arousal.

"I thought we were going to make love first."

"I changed my mind," he snapped. "I have no use for you."

Gwen said nothing.

He came up behind her, holding the knife to her delicate throat, his hands shaking as he did so.

"One more chance, my sweet. Tell me who you work for. Betray your country. Just one tiny little piece of information. Anything I can put to good use. Perhaps who is decoding the ciphers? Say the word and I'll set you free."

"Freedom is in the eye of the beholder. I would be physically free, but my heart would be imprisoned with guilt. If you must kill me, do so."

Stunned, Hunter gripped the knife closer to her neck. She gasped. He swore, and then cut her ropes and pulled her blindfold off.

"I'm sorry," he said in English.

Gwen looked up, tears brimming in her eyes. "You will be."

CHAPTER NINE

Wolf—
I would apologize for breaking your nose. But I'm not sorry. Besides, it was more of a snout, and you deserved every broken bone for holding a knife to my throat. Do it again and I'll hold a knife to... well, use your imagination.

—Red

FURIOUS, GWEN COULD ONLY look at Hunter in shock. The cad had kidnapped her! Tortured her! What the devil was wrong with him? And why had he done it? Why the kissing? Why the... touching?

"You're insane," she blurted as she jumped from the chair, while simultaneously pulling a knife from her sleeve.

His eyes went wide he lifted his hands in front of him. "I had to be sure."

"What about trust?" She thrust the knife into the air.

Hunter continued to back up. "I trust no one."

"Could have told me that before you tried to kill me!"

Hunter laughed. The man laughed! "I would never have

killed you, my sweet." He winked. "I was merely testing you. You passed, by the way."

"Oh." Gwen laughed. "I passed, well, fantastic! That makes it all worth it, now, doesn't it?"

"Yes?" Hunter lifted an eyebrow and made his way toward the door.

"Don't you dare," Gwen ordered as he reached for the lock. Like a typical man, he didn't listen, nor did he take her threat seriously. So she threw the knife at his hand.

And missed it by an inch.

Hunter cursed a blue streak and glared at her. "You could have stabbed me!"

"If I had meant to stab you, my knife would be buried in your neck up to its hilt, Wolf." Gwen lunged for him, angrier than she had ever been in her entire life.

Hunter wasn't a typical agent. He didn't shy away from female spies. No, instead he fought back. Which intrigued her more than she was willing to admit.

He threw her against the wall, grabbing her hands and pinning them above her head. "I had to be certain."

"You could have just held me at gunpoint. You didn't have to kiss me! Or, or touch me!"

Hunter's eyes went dark as he leaned in and sniffed her neck again. "Yes, yes I did."

Gwen went still. His scent, his touch, everything about him was overwhelming her good sense. Her lips tingled with the memory of his scorching kiss.

"You hurt me," she mumbled as he held her in place.

"Then allow me to kiss and make it better."

She had no time to respond as Hunter bent down and kissed her neck. A hungry growl erupted from his lips, and he pushed his body against hers.

Gwen bit at his lip. He cursed but continued to kiss her. "I hate you," she murmured.

"I hate you too," he agreed, and his tongue chose that exact moment to plunge into her mouth and greedily take possession.

Her body jerked against him, wrenching free of his grasp. "This needs to stop. We've crossed so many lines..."

"Forget the lines. I never was one to follow rules anyway." Hunter released her hands and lifted her into his arms. She had no choice but to cling to him as he continued to do wicked things with his tongue, things no debutante should experience on her first come out.

"Stop," she said breathlessly.

Hunter released her. They simultaneously stepped back from one another.

"I've been very... er..."

"I think the word you are looking for is *bad*. You've been very bad, and clearly you're losing your mind."

"That, too." Hunter ran a hand through his hair. "The thing is..." He paced in front of her. "I cannot just have one taste. The more I taste, the more I want."

"And when did you first realize you had a drinking problem?"

Hunter's head snapped up. He rolled his eyes. "If only it were a problem that could be solved with drink."

"Am I the problem?" Gwen asked as she clenched her dress between her hands. Unable to trust herself to keep from touching him if her hands were not occupied. He was too beautiful. Firelight danced off his high cheekbones and his eyes. Those eyes that women nearly fainted over. Golden brown eyes stared back at her through dark sooty lashes. A woman could experience the greatest of pleasure if only she looked into his eyes. For his gaze was like a physical caress.

"Yes."

"Pardon?"

"You asked if you were the problem, and you are. Now

that I've had a taste, I do not think I can keep myself from hunting you."

Gwen noted the seriousness in his voice. "Are you sure you have good enough equipment to engage in such a hunt? We wouldn't want you to... misfire."

Hunter groaned.

Gwen smiled. "Yes, I believe it is my turn to torture you. Take a good hard look, Hunter."

His eyes scanned her hungrily from head to toe. She took a step toward him and grabbed his hand, placing it on her shoulder and running it down her chest.

"You have not earned the right, the privilege, the honor, to touch me. Next time you do so without permission, I will throw my knife, and believe me, it will be right on target."

He squinted his eyes. "Do you truly think you are strong enough to withstand temptation?"

"Who says I'm tempted?"

"Your eyes betray you."

"Funny." Gwen leaned in and whispered, "I was just going to say the same thing about you." She turned to walk toward the door until she felt Hunter's hand tug her arm. Without thinking, she whipped around and punched him in the nose.

Hunter fell to the floor and cursed.

"Good night, Wolf."

"Red," he grumbled from the floor, but this time he did not chase after her.

CHAPTER TEN

Red—

Use my imagination? Surely I did not read that correctly! For you to give my mind free rein when it comes to you, sweetheart? Well, let us just say that is a dangerous game to play. Guess what I'm imagining right now...

—Wolf

HUNTER WOKE THE FOLLOWING day with a pounding headache. Most likely from the bottle of brandy needed to numb the pain from the night previous.

He quickly rang for his valet and joined everyone for breakfast.

Every bone in his body felt stiff and his muscles sore. The last thing he wanted to do today was see Gwen, but he needed to be among her admirers. Chances were, if they knew the right hook she packed, they wouldn't go anywhere near her house.

Stupid wench. A blasted broken nose! How the devil was he to explain that?

"Got in a fight, did you?" Dominique said upon entering the dining room and examining Hunter's face.

"Yes. A large fellow was upset with me."

Isabelle waltzed into the room, only overhearing the last part. "What did he do, punch you?" Her eyes fell to Hunter's nose. "Oh my! Does it hurt?"

Hunter grinned. "Terribly so."

"You poor, poor man! Who would do this to you?"

"A beast of a man with a good right hook," Hunter lied, and turned his gaze upon Isabelle. "It hurts very much."

"No." Dominique shook his head and yelled louder. "Hunter, my wife will not nurse you back to health, you fool. Now sit down before I give you another reason to be howling with pain."

Smirking, Hunter walked to his seat.

The butler announced another guest but Hunter ignored his presence, mainly because the throbbing behind his nose was so intense, he wanted to drown in a bottle of brandy.

"I hope I'm not too late!" Gwen announced.

Coffee spewed out of Hunter's mouth, landing directly on Dominique's face.

"Please excuse Hunter," Dominique said, wiping remnants of coffee from his face. "It seems he was in a fight with a large man last night and has yet to recover his senses."

Hunter groaned aloud.

Isabelle sighed. "Oh, it must pain you so much!"

He prayed the ground would swallow him whole.

Gwen gave him a saucy grin. "My, my, that bruised quite nicely. How tragic that you look less handsome this morning than you did last night. How big was the man, did you say?"

"Yes, tell us exactly what happened!" Isabelle turned toward him, her eyes full of worry.

Cursing Gwen to perdition, Hunter gritted his teeth. "I was walking along the street when all of a sudden—"

"Which street?" Gwen interrupted.

"The one..." Hunter shook his head to clear it. "The one outside." He inwardly cringed.

"Did he hit his head as well?" Gwen asked, taking a seat. "Hunter," she directed her attention back toward him, "was it the street in front of Montmouth's house?"

He was an absolute idiot. "Why yes, I believe so."

Gwen nodded.

Isabelle and Dominique sat in silence, waiting for the rest of the lie, no doubt.

"So, you were walking down the street?" Isabelle finally patted his arm.

"Yes, when out of nowhere someone jumped out of the bushes and—"

"—there are no bushes in front of Montmouth's house," Gwen pointed out.

Hunter cursed. "Perhaps you should tell the story, my dear, considering you seem to remember it so much better than I?"

Isabelle gasped. "You were with him! Oh, sister, weren't you frightened?"

"Terrified," Gwen said through clenched teeth.

Hunter grinned even though it hurt like the devil. *Let's watch her talk her way out of this.*

"But imagine my surprise..." Gwen lifted the cup of tea to her lips and blew softly across it, making what truly was his favorite anatomical part flare to life. "When the large man merely stole some of Hunter's money and continued down the road. Strangest thing, for Hunter refused to fight back. Something about being a lover, not so much a fighter. Isn't that right, Hunter?" Gwen smiled sweetly and winked.

He was going to kill her.

No, he was going to tie her to a chair and then...

Blast. He needed to stop his imagination before it got out

of hand.

"Er, yes," he grumbled.

Dominique tilted his head. "Then who was the gentleman that gave you the black eye?"

Hunter opened his mouth to respond, but Gwen beat him to it. "Oh, silly man, how could you forget?" She laughed. Everyone joined in even though they had no idea why they were mocking him, yet it seemed Gwen did. He couldn't wait to hear the ending to her sordid tale. Would she explain her involvement?

He took a sip of coffee and waited.

"I punched him."

The liquid, of course, spewed out of his mouth for the second time that morning, as well as every curse underneath the sun, causing Isabelle to turn red and Dominique to push back his chair as he jerked to his feet.

"Gwen?" Dominique looked between the two of them. "Whyever would you punch him? And Hunter, I'm dreadfully sorry for saying so, but what a wonderful right hook you must have, my dear!"

Gwen beamed. "Thank you."

"Yes, let us all applaud her for assault." Hunter clapped loudly and groaned, leaning his head onto his hands.

"He tried to kiss me," Gwen blurted.

Isabelle gasped and then burst out laughing.

"What!" Dominique roared as he stomped toward Hunter and grabbed at the lapels of his smart jacket.

"Ah, so the Beast returns," Hunter joked, though truly he was expecting Dominique to blacken his eye as well. He even turned his face just slightly so the Beast would hit the right instead of the left. After all, the left was his good side.

"I'm not going to hit you."

"He screams like a girl when you do," Gwen helpfully added.

Hunter cursed again.

"Cease cursing in front of gently bred ladies," Dominique growled, releasing him.

"Calling the kettle a bit black, are we?" Hunter smirked, then took a step back as Dominique lunged for him again.

"Why her? Out of all the women you can dally with."

Gwen began choking. Isabelle hit her across the back.

"Why my sister-in-law?"

"It was dark."

The room fell silent.

"Pardon?" Dominique's eyes widened. "That is to be your excuse? It was dark? What, pray tell, were you trying to do, then? And how did it turn into a kiss?"

"Assault," Gwen said. "It was more of an assault."

"Helpful," Hunter muttered. "Oh, calm down, Dominique. Truly I meant no harm. I thought she wasn't breathing. I was merely trying to help."

"By kissing her?" Isabelle piped up, her grin wider than that of the cat that got the cream.

"Why, yes. Thought it would shock her system and all that."

"And why wouldn't she be breathing?" Dominique clearly felt the need to ask something intelligent.

"After the robbery, she panicked. You know women, they tend to get all out of sorts when there is danger. I believe she even screamed." He peered around Dominique and saw Gwen roll her eyes. "Truthfully, you should thank me."

"For?" Dominique was incredulous.

Hunter grinned smugly. "Saving her life."

Isabelle cleared her throat. "Thank you." She truly was the sweetest woman, and the only one to tame Dominique. He glared at her, and she glared back, standing her ground, then nodded toward her husband.

Dominique's eyes narrowed at Hunter. He leaned in and

whispered into his ear, "If you touch her again, I shall kill you and bury the body in Russia."

Hunter felt himself pale, mainly because he could see his friend doing it. Dominique's family had all but betrayed him, and his father had tried to kill him twice, so his remaining family was immensely important, and he was fiercely protective, which suited Montmouth's needs just fine, considering he was no longer the only protector of the three sisters.

"Have I made myself clear?" Dominique asked.

"Crystal." Hunter squirmed beneath his stare and went back to his seat. Gwen smirked at him and winked.

He smirked back, made sure Isabelle and Dominique wouldn't be the wiser, and then licked his lips and blew her a kiss.

She turned red.

He bit his bottom lip, allowing his gaze to travel down the expanse of her dress in approval, then looked away.

They finished breakfast in what could only be described as a pregnant silence, where Dominique took special care to play with the knife on the table and Isabelle glared at her husband every time it clanked against a glass.

Gwen chose to ignore Hunter completely, which irritated him. How could she ignore him when he was having the devil of a time keeping his gaze away from her perfection?

Pride told him it was because he looked like he'd had a fight with the devil and lost. Perhaps women weren't attracted to men they could successfully punch.

"Gwen, are you taking callers this afternoon?" Dominique asked, clearing his throat in the awkward silence.

Gwen stole a glance at Hunter then looked down at her lap. "Why yes, I believe I will be receiving callers at Montmouth's residence. I do hope some men show up. After all, I desire a husband above all else." She blushed convincingly and ducked her head like an innocent virgin, which of course made Hunter think of all the ways his body was willing to rid her of said virginity.

Hunter flexed his hand, causing the fork to clatter to the floor. He mumbled his apologies and quickly picked up the discarded silver.

Dominique smiled genuinely at Gwen. "I'm sure you will be the toast of the ton."

"Yes, I'm sure," Hunter said dryly.

"What has gotten into you?" Dominique snapped.

"Forgive him," Gwen intervened. "After all, Hunter had a rough night. Not many men escape my presence unscathed."

There was too much truth to that statement.

"And we cannot all be as clever as wolves when it comes to escape, now, can we, Hunter?"

Isabelle looked at Gwen curiously. Dominique did the same. Hunter wanted to laugh. The girl had no idea that both of his dear friends knew of his current involvement with the War Office, as well as his plans this Season. She was doing nothing more than causing them to be suspicious of her.

So he added more. "But of course, if a woman in a red cloak was to lead me down the path, I would have no choice but to follow her out, in hopes that she wouldn't lead me astray."

"Red is the color of treason."

"No, my dear." Hunter grinned. "It is the color of lust."

Her eyes narrowed.

Dominique lifted his eyes heavenward.

But Hunter kept his eyes trained on Gwen. A challenge had just been given. He was not about to run away from a tiny woman. No matter how much of a punch she possessed. No, he was going to hunt her, he was going to chase her, and make her wish she had never awakened the Wolf in the first place.

With a cheerful smile, he lifted the coffee to his lips and

chuckled. He had plans to make.

CHAPTER ELEVEN

Wolf—

Imaginations are a funny thing. For this moment, I am imagining you being shot with my favorite pistol. Do tell, how many duels have you had to fight because of your lack of self-control? After all, wolves are rarely known for their restraint, and I believe I've experienced that firsthand.

—Red

GWEN DONNED HER AFTERNOON gown and sat demurely on the sofa. Isabelle had begged to join her during her first day receiving callers. The three sisters sat in relative silence as they waited for the first gentleman to arrive. According to Rosalind, flowers had been delivered all morning; they now littered the blue salon, making her eyes water.

Weren't flowers supposed to make a woman swoon? Or perhaps smile? It did nothing except fill her with disgust. None of these men knew her, knew who she really was, or the things she had put herself through for the wellbeing of her family.

She sighed and took a sip of hot tea.

Goode, their butler, walked in and cleared his throat. "My lady, you have callers. The Earl of Trehmont and Viscount Redding."

Lovely.

"Gentlemen." Rosalind rose and greeted both men. In Gwen's eyes, Rosalind was by far the most graceful woman she had ever encountered. She was also strong, unyielding. Isabelle was similar. With golden brown hair and bright blue eyes, she was every man's fantasy. Whereas Gwen, well, Gwen was nothing. At least she felt like nothing when she sat next to her sisters.

The only time she had ever felt beautiful had been when Hunter kissed her upon their first meeting. And look where that had led her, down a dark path of lust-filled gazes and promises of seduction.

Redding was the first to speak up. "I do hope you've received my flowers, my lady. And may I say how lovely you look this afternoon?"

You may not. Gwen felt her nostrils flare. "Yes, and thank you. How kind of you to say so."

Trehmont flinched next to Redding. "Lady Gwendolyn, are you possibly available for an afternoon ride through the park tomorrow?"

No. I'd rather allow Hunter to trap me against a chair again. "Of course." She forced her face to break into a smile. "That would be wonderful."

Isabelle elbowed her sister. Perhaps she was doing it a bit brown. She grimaced.

"Are you in pain?" Trehmont blurted.

If only he knew that his very presence made her feel ill. His hair was slicked back with gobs of something — she had never seen such material in a man's hair. His jacket a bit too tight, and his smile lecherous. If he tried to kiss her, she was going to murder him.

"The Royal Duke of Haverstone," Goode announced, as Hunter bounded into the room. With a flourish, he sat near Gwen and snatched a biscuit from the nearby table.

Never had she been so thankful for the Wolf to appear.

"Blast, but these are wonderful biscuits. Tell me." Hunter ignored the men and turned to Gwen. "Does your cook possess some sort of magic or does she merely add a bit of your sweetness to the delicacy?" He licked his lips and took another bite.

Rosalind coughed. Gwen had to bite her lip to keep from grinning from ear to ear. The fool.

"Ahem." Trehmont stumbled over his words. "I was just announcing to my valet this morning of your beauty, my lady."

"Valet." Hunter laughed. "Didn't know you still possessed the blunt to employ one, Trehmont."

Gwen's mouth dropped open as she tried to think quickly of what to say to diffuse the situation. She looked between the two men.

Trehmont's face turned a purplish shade of red before he squirmed in his seat. "I'm happy to announce I've come into a bit of a more comfortable situation. Surely enough to provide for a beautiful young lady."

"Is that so?" Redding suddenly perked up, seeming quite interested in this sudden change of information. "And how, may I ask, has your situation improved?"

Rosalind laughed lightly. "Gentlemen, is this truly a place for such talk?"

"Of course not." Hunter grinned wickedly at Gwen. "Might I say that gown is terribly awful on you."

"Pardon?" Gwen gaped. "Apologies, but it seems your attempt at humor has missed its mark."

"It was not an attempt, and I believe I hit my mark quite

well." He turned toward the two gentlemen. "I am, after all, an excellent marksman."

"So we've heard." Redding glared.

"At any rate, allow me to explain myself." Hunter cleared his throat and leaned forward. "That particular gown is a pretty enough gown, but in my mind it detracts away from the poetry of your face. The angle of your soft jaw, the billowy softness of your lips against that pale skin. Those are the things a man wishes to focus on, not gowns."

Gwen squirmed in her seat. Never had a man been so forward. Unfortunately, the warmth she felt was entirely false. Hunter might desire her, in a lust-filled selfish way, but he cared nothing for her heart. In fact, she was convinced she would never find a man who would.

Which was why this entire farce was almost as painful as it was difficult. It was akin to giving a child a beautiful new pony and then at the last minute ripping it out of their hands.

She nodded in his direction and took a sip of tea to collect her thoughts. "Your attempt at flattery confuses me, but I thank you nonetheless. No doubt it took you days to come up with such a compliment, and even then it fell flat."

Trehmont began to laugh. "Doesn't mince words, does she?"

Redding joined in.

Hunter, however, did not take his eyes off of Gwen.

"Say, my lady," Redding spoke up. "Since you seem to be occupied with Trehmont tomorrow afternoon, would you be agreeable to a chaperoned walk in the park Monday?"

"I would be honored." Gwen tried to keep herself from glaring at Redding. Something about him gave her pause, though she had no idea why.

She sighed.

"Perfect." Redding rubbed his hands together and leaned forward.

Rosalind seemed to let out a deep exhale next to her. Most likely in relief, considering she had been so worried about Gwen ever since her return from Dominique's castle.

If only her sisters knew. Her innocence had long ago been taken, by watching the horrors of what men with power could do. Not a night went by when she didn't see the nightmares of the torture Napoleon had inflicted on some of his people, women in general. She had barely escaped without becoming another conquest.

And the Crown had done nothing to commend her except send her back into the darkness of Hades in order to glean more information.

She was broken. Perhaps Hunter was right. She was a temptation for a man, but that was all. For she could offer nothing, save her body, to another human being, for who wanted a soul that was so tainted?

CHAPTER TWELVE

Red—

You truly looked beautiful today. I didn't mean to upset you. I was trying to goad the men into defending you. Lecherous idiots that they are. Do tell me what you learn after you spend your afternoons with both of them, and do not, I repeat, do not allow them to get you alone. Take a chaperone, or you will force the Wolf to become the Hunter, and we both know what happens when the Hunter is after you...

—Wolf

HUNTER SHIFTED UNCOMFORTABLY IN his seat as all three gentlemen sent dirty looks in his direction. Words flew freely from his mouth without his brain once discussing with his lips what should or should not come out. It was as if he had taken complete leave of his senses. What the devil had he been thinking? Perhaps Dominique had drugged him for kissing Gwen. If the Beast only knew that it had been several kisses and he had in fact captured and tortured her.

The image of his body floating face-down in the river

wasn't even enough to keep him from wanting to slap himself for his foolish words.

For him, a man of excellent seduction skills, to tell a woman in front of other men, no less, that she looked awful! He'd nearly groaned when he saw her face fall. Her dress *was* awful. It had nothing to do with what was beneath it, but it was entirely too proper for his liking.

He liked her in red.

Curse the woman.

Now every time he saw her, she seemed to be wearing some ugly color that made him want to rip the dress from her frame.

Which his body quite agreed with.

Though he imagined her sisters wouldn't have been pleased with him. In some ways, he was angry with Gwen. She was a temptation he could not afford, not with the lives of people he cared about in the balance. Yet there she was, a conundrum if there ever was one.

It made him uneasy to see Trehmont and Redding in the drawing room and even more nervous that Gwen would be spending time with them. Yet the plan was working perfectly. Both men seemed entranced by her. Who would not be? Considering they were being pressured to settle down this Season, it was hardly difficult to get the men to fawn over her. Now at least it would be easier to follow them and keep a watchful eye on their actions. His nose suddenly pained him; he reached up and touched it. At least he knew she could defend herself.

The tea became cold in his cup. He put it down on the table and rose to excuse himself, when the butler entered again.

"The Earl of Eastbrook."

Trapped, with no way to escape, Hunter sat back down.

Redding and Trehmont seemed less than pleased that

they had more competition, for Eastbrook had taken great care in making his appearance perfect. Stupid man. All Hunter needed was his cousin sniffing around Gwen's skirts; he had enough problems as it was.

"Ah Haverstone, thought I might find you here!" Eastbrook slapped his gloves against his leg and smiled coolly. Then his eyes fell on Gwen. "And what a lovely creature, more lovely than even my best dreams."

Gwen blushed.

Why the devil did she blush?

Could she not see how evil he was?

Well, perhaps he wasn't particularly evil. After all, he hadn't necessarily done anything but set himself up quite nicely within society. Treat his friends with respect and keep from vices like gambling and heavy drink.

Which, if you asked Hunter, meant he was a terrible human being. What man didn't engage in at least one vice or two? It was the quiet fellows a gentleman had to worry about. He narrowed his eyes in his cousin's direction.

"Thank you," Gwen answered, folding her hands in her lap.

If it was at all possible, Hunter's eyes narrowed even more as he watched his cousin smile seductively at Gwen. Hunter imagined his hands around his cousin's neck and suddenly felt calm enough to breathe again.

"...Did you hear nothing I just said?" Eastbrook addressed Hunter.

No, apologies, I was busy strategically planning your murder. Perhaps at the end of a pistol rather than my bare hands? Too messy. He cleared his throat and smiled. "What was it that you asked?"

"Have you seen Lainhart yet?"

The entire room seemed to take a sudden inhalation, making it impossible for Hunter to focus on anything except steadying the ramming of his heart against his chest. Why did the blasted man have to mention his grandfather again, especially in front of his former employees?

"He's dying," Eastbrook continued.

"Oh, that poor man!" Gwen patted Eastbrook's hand. Hunter clenched his fist. "Whatever is the matter with him?"

"I imagine it is severe disappointment," Redding piped up.

"Disappointment?" Gwen tilted her head.

"Why, yes." Redding leaned forward, but not before his gaze quickly went to Hunter in what could only be described as a smug look. "His grandson by marriage is, after all, a disgrace."

"A disgrace, you say?" Gwen looked uncomfortably between Hunter and Redding. Eastbrook reached for her hand. If he did that one more time, Hunter was going to remove it with a rusty fork.

Trehmont had the audacity to laugh, as if he wasn't a stain upon his own family name, the lecher. "But of course, haven't you heard?"

"I'm sure if she hasn't, it is only a matter of time," Hunter said smoothly.

The drawing room was entirely too small for that much testosterone, Hunter knew that much. If one more man puffed out his chest, they would look like those ridiculous emperor penguins waddling around their mates.

Goode walked in again, this time with a grim expression on his face. Had all the gentlemen decided to call at the same time?

"Sir Hollins to call."

Hollins swept into the room with a flourish, making a ridiculous spectacle of handing his hat and gloves to Goode before sitting on the already-too-miniscule sofa near Trehmont. "Ah, Lady Gwendolyn, you are a thing of beauty."

"So I've been told," she murmured to herself, but Hunter caught it. Fighting a smile, he looked straight through Hollins as if he were the most meaningless rat on the planet and then looked away, hoping his point had been made.

"I say." Hollins chuckled uncomfortably. "Seems tense in here. Do tell what has everyone in such silence."

Hunter grabbed another biscuit and chomped on it quite loudly, then threw his arm over the side of the sofa and grinned. "Why, my many sins. Care to join in, Hollins? After all, I'm sure your embellishments will be quite helpful in steering the dear lady away from my advances."

Hollins tugged at his cravat. "I believe you make enough of a spectacle of yourself without my embellishments helping, your grace." The way he said *grace* almost sounded like a hiss from his lips.

"Let us not speak of it anymore," Rosalind piped up. Hunter had almost forgotten the two sisters were even present. What they must think of him now. Even Isabelle did not know of his disgrace.

"No, let's," Hunter said, voice hoarse. "Say what you came to say." This he directed at Eastbrook, whose eyes revealed years of hatred.

"No, my ladies, this tale is too sordid for drawing room conversation. Wouldn't you rather talk about the weather, or the lovely Season?"

"Or the rumor that we have a traitor within our midst! Apparently, and you did not hear this from me, but someone has been selling information to the French," Gwen piped up.

All heads turned to her.

She nodded just slightly to Hunter.

He swallowed the knot of emotion in his throat. It seemed Red had saved the Wolf, from himself and from further disgrace. He found he could not even meet her gaze as he looked down at his hands, which were now trembling in his lap from years of pent-up anger and guilt.

Trehmont sputtered as Eastbrook leaned in to grab a biscuit. "My lady, that is not at all proper information, nor is it true."

"Oh." Gwen tilted her head and shrugged. "I overheard some of the servants, or was it Redding discussing something of the sort? I'm sure it was nothing." She smiled and waved into the air.

Redding's face turned pale as he looked at all the gentleman. "Well, on that note, I believe it is time for me to go. Apparently I've gone mad, to make up such silly lies." He bowed to the ladies, and went to kiss Gwen's hand. "I look forward to our walk through the park Monday afternoon."

Hunter noticed Redding's hand was clenching Gwen's quite forcefully. He was ready to jump to her rescue when Eastbrook suddenly jerked to his feet, nearly knocking Redding away, considering how close in proximity they were.

"Oh, apologies." Eastbrook looked anything but apologetic. Interesting indeed that he would be so perceptive of Gwen's discomfort. Hunter wasn't sure if he should be grateful or irritated. He decided on both.

"Let us have that wonderful discussion over a glass of whiskey," Eastbrook addressed Hunter. Reluctantly, he rose from his seat and followed his cousin out of the house.

Hunter wasn't sure why he felt such a glutton for punishment, nor why he had even agreed to this ridiculous meeting. He ordered a whiskey and took a seat next to the famous bay window of White's.

The same window that had witnessed men lose entire fortunes. For who was stupid enough to bet how many people would walk by and what type of hats they would be wearing?

Hunter drank greedily from the glass and sighed. Eastbrook took a seat opposite him and glared.

"At least allow me the pleasure of being foxed, so when you attempt to murder me, it won't aggravate my nose."

Eastbrook smirked. "Got yourself into a little scratch, did you?"

A vision of Gwen flashed through Hunter's mind. A scratch? Did that make her a kitten? Blast, what he wouldn't give to be the man to help her retract those claws. He shifted uncomfortably and smirked into his glass before answering, "You could say that."

An awkward silence followed, if one could ever call White's silent.

"You must make amends before he dies."

"For what?" Hunter all but yelled, as the pain of that day came back full force and hit him squarely in the chest. "Don't you think I know it was my fault?"

Eastbrook said nothing, so Hunter continued. "Have I not suffered enough? I am a shell of a man." He hadn't meant to say that part aloud.

Eastbrook reared back as if he had just been slapped. Hunter cursed and went to order another whiskey. When he returned, Eastbrook was looking out the window.

"Do you remember when we first met?"

Hunter cringed. "Do not tell me you are becoming sentimental."

"Do you remember?" Eastbrook looked at him and grinned. "I told you I was going to grow up and marry a beautiful woman, and that when she said yes I would howl like a wolf does unto the moon. I would howl with excitement, with pleasure."

"We were but lads." Hunter felt the need to clear his throat of the emotion that now clogged it.

"You said if I was a wolf, then you and Ash would be the

wolf's companions. We would grow up, marry beautiful women, and howl together at the moon in our excitement."

Hunter hadn't heard his brother's name on anyone's lips for ten years. It hurt more than he'd realized it would.

"The three of us, we were best friends."

"And then I ruined it. Was that what you were going to say?" Voice hoarse, Hunter had to look away to keep himself from lashing out.

"No," Eastbrook said calmly. "I was going to say, you abandoned the dream."

Unable to believe his ears, Hunter jerked back toward Eastbrook. "I had no choice! In one blasted day I lost the love of my life and my only remaining blood relation. Tell me, if you are so wise, cousin, what would you have done?"

Eastbrook sighed. "I wouldn't have shamed my family by abandoning them when they needed me most. I wouldn't refuse to respond to letters. I wouldn't disappear without a trace. I wouldn't leave a dying old man without saying goodbye, and I sure as fire would not have disgraced my dead wife's memory by screwing the first whore that smiled at me."

Hunter focused on a tiny speck on the window. It was the only way to keep himself from killing his cousin with his bare hands. He had no idea of Hunter's pain. How dare he judge him! He hadn't been there. He hadn't seen the blood. Oh, the blood.

He swallowed another gulp of whiskey and put his mask firmly back into place before looking back at his cousin. "You're boring me. Are we done?"

"Yes." Eastbrook's eyes narrowed. "But you need to visit him. Promise me, if our past friendship meant anything to you, promise me you'll visit him. And soon."

"Fine," Hunter said hastily. "I'll visit him first thing Monday morning, if that pleases you. But you will do me a favor in return."

"Do you truly think you are in a position to be asking me a favor?"

"Yes." With a smug grin, Hunter raised his glass to his lips. "I believe I am."

Eastbrook nodded, just once. "Let's have it."

"Stay away from her."

"I'm sorry, you are going to need to be more specific as to who you are referring to."

"Lady Gwendolyn. Stay away from her."

Eastbrook swallowed the rest of his whiskey and set the glass on the table in front of them. Without answering, he turned and walked toward the door, then seemed to think better about it and stole a glance back at Hunter. "Do not ask me to make promises I cannot keep."

"She is..." Hunter couldn't very well say *mine*. That sounded possessive. Yet all he wanted to do was slug his cousin across the jaw for the condescending smile pasted on his face.

"She is what?" With a laugh, Eastbrook walked out of the establishment, leaving Hunter alone and very much wanting to murder the next person that dared speak to him.

"Fancy seeing you here."

He knew that voice. Please let it not be true. Please let him be already foxed and conjuring up dukes.

He looked to his left and saw Montmouth with another fellow in tow. God was surely punishing him. He hadn't the temper to talk with Montmouth longer than two seconds.

Hunter imagined his body would be thrown through the glass window if he engaged in a longer conversation.

"May we sit?" Montmouth motioned to the two empty chairs. Hunter quickly took a long swig of his drink.

"Rawlings, do take a seat. You look positively ill."

The man with dark features, named Rawlings, sat on the chair but looked like he was ready to either murder someone or strangle himself, his hands were wrung so tightly.

"This..." Montmouth pointed to Rawlings, who was now staring at the floor as if it were to come alive at any moment. Was he foxed? "This is Lord Rawlings. His wife at this very instant has kicked him from his home so she may bring his heir into the world without him pacing the floorboards, most likely ruining the new floors in the process."

That explained his ill look.

For whatever reason, Hunter took pity. "I'm sure she will do nicely."

Rawlings' head snapped up.

Instant recognition flashed across his features.

Truly, Hunter should have looked away or at least said something, but all he could do was sputter. "Phillip!"

"Hunter!"

"What?" Montmouth's reaction was filled with more dread then excitement.

Hunter jumped to his feet and pumped Phillip's hand with glee. "I haven't seen you since France!"

"Yes, about that..." Phillip turned slightly red and glanced back at Montmouth before scratching his head and shifting his feet. "Not many know the sordid details."

"It was you!" Montmouth nearly shouted.

"Shh!" both men said in unison, all three of them now taking their seats and huddling together.

Monmouth looked between the two of them and finally addressed Phillip. "He was the one that bet you to swim naked in France?"

"Nothing but rumors." Hunter tried to defend him but failed miserably.

Rawlings shook his head, shoulders finally relaxing. He leaned back and laughed. "In his defense, the man was drunk when he bet me."

"And in his defense..." Hunter joined with them in

laughter. "He was drunker, and if I remember correctly, gaining a little too much attention from a certain courtesan who would have robbed him blind if given the opportunity."

"And there's also that." Rawlings laughed. "It is good to see you, Hunter. Or shall I address you as Haverstone? It's odd, really, I hadn't ever thought about your title before."

"Yes, well, I didn't even know you had inherited until now, so you are forgiven."

Montmouth was glancing between the two as if he had just created some grievous sin. His face had turned pale. "How do you two know one another?"

"He's a spy," Phillip blurted and then quickly looked to Hunter. Who nodded his head in amusement.

"Pardon?" Montmouth hooted with laughter. His head fell back against the chair as he wiped tears from his eyes.

Hunter fought the urge to shout his own name aloud in order to gain attention, for he truly was that famous. How had Montmouth not heard of him? Or at least put two and two together?

"Glad I amuse you," Hunter said dryly, for once not putting his foolish smile or rakish lazy mask in place.

Montmouth looked at him, really looked at him. Hunter waited and tilted his head.

"I don't understand."

It was time for Phillip to laugh. "Surely you jest! You truly did not know that you've been waltzing around with the Wolf?"

"Wolf?" Montmouth said, then his eyes widened. "*The* Wolf?"

"The one and only." Hunter saluted.

Montmouth looked between the two of them. "But he's an idiot." This directed at Phillip.

"He's brilliant." Phillip defended his old friend and rose to his feet. "This truly has been a pleasure. I hadn't thought to see you again. By the by, thank you for keeping me out of trouble in France."

"Not a problem." And Hunter meant it.

"Do call upon us soon." Phillip smiled and pumped his hand. "Wish me luck. I'm off to meet my son or daughter."

"Son," Hunter said without realizing he had spoken. Both men looked at him. "A man like you deserves a son."

Phillip nodded and walked off.

"Explain yourself," Montmouth growled before Hunter could even find his seat again.

"No."

"No?"

"Are you deaf?"

"Are you stupid?" Montmouth fired back.

"Clearly not. But I take it you are."

"I'm ignoring that slight to my intelligence, but only because I'm interested in what you're doing back in London and living with Dominique and Isabelle."

Hunter opened his mouth to speak but Montmouth interrupted him. "And dancing with Gwen. Oh, please tell me you haven't made advances toward her. A spy? I'm to protect them. I'm to—"

"Stop." Hunter groaned, suddenly feeling a headache coming on. "I don't have time to speak of it. Just know I would do nothing to harm your sisters, any of them."

"Fine," Montmouth bit out. "Be sure that you don't."

Hunter placed his glass on the table and shrugged. "Not to worry. I'm retired. I have only the purest intentions."

"Says the wolf to the sheep."

"Only the stupid ones."

Montmouth cursed. "Promise to leave the innocent ones alone? Pick off the weak, the feeble-minded, the ones who have it coming, but leave Gwen alone."

Hunter knew he couldn't promise anything of the sort, so

he nodded his head and looked away. "On that note." Hunter rose. "It's been a trying day."

Montmouth nodded to Hunter as he left.

Trying day indeed. He did not even feel himself fall asleep that night as he lay in bed at Dominique's house, but he did remember the woman he saw before he closed his eyes. A lady in red.

CHAPTER THIRTEEN

Wolf—

I know you may find this hard to bite, but considering you're a wolf, I'll just encourage you to act on instinct. I can very well take care of myself. And if you need proof, by all means examine your nose in the mirror. If the purple and yellow stains across your features aren't enough evidence to my case, then allow me to once again show you how worthy of an opponent I truly am.

—Red

"YOUR EYES ARE LIKE flowers."

Gwen blinked rapidly; perhaps she could cause herself to faint if she did so?

"Your hair like spun..." Oh, this should be good. The man coughed. "Spun wool."

Gwen smiled. "Like a sheep?"

"A black sheep," he confirmed. *Baah*. The man turned red.

She could only refer to him as *man* because he had been the fifteenth man to come calling and by then she had come up

113

with nicknames for every male present. She'd quit listening to their names after the third caller. This one she called *man*, because truly there was nothing identifying about him. He was average height, average weight, and most likely average intelligence, at least so she'd thought.

And then he compared her hair to wool.

"Yes, well, I do love farm animals." Gwen truly didn't know what else to say. Rosalind had quit the room hours ago while Isabelle still sat poised at Gwen's side. Poor dear. If Gwen was tempted to jump out the window or slip and fall on a table so she'd have a blunt head wound, she could not even begin to imagine her sister's trauma at having to live through this with her.

"You do!" the man shouted and clapped his hands. Clapped. As if he had just witnessed a play. "I always say that the best wife is one who appreciates God's creatures."

"Yes, well—"

"Do you cook?" He leaned forward and licked his lips.

Gwen eyed the cane behind him and wondered how fast the man could move if she were to strike him with it. "No, I'm a gently bred lady."

"Oh, of course." He tugged at the sleeve of his too-tight jacket and winced. "I was merely making conversation and my house, well, it is in the country and I do not exactly have the funds to keep a cook full time, so when we marry—"

Presumptuous squatty little man! "I'm going to have to bid you good afternoon. The light grows dark, and I promised my sister I would attend her house for dinner this evening."

The man looked to Isabelle and grinned. He couldn't be waiting for an invitation, could he? Of all the fool-hearted notions!

"Y-yes." Isabelle smiled sweetly. "We are to meet with my husband, the Beast of Russia. I'm sure you've heard of him."

"The Beast." Merciful heavens, why the devil were the man's hands trembling? Was he going to wet himself as well?

"Yes." Gwen nodded urgently. "And he is ever so cross when we are late."

"Oh, well then, I'll just..." The man jerked out of his seat and walked briskly out the door.

"Well." Isabelle huffed.

Gwen felt a headache push through her temples. "Listen to me very carefully, Isabelle."

"Sister, if I have to listen to anyone talk for another minute, including you, my head shall explode on the spot."

Gwen ignored her. "It is imperative that you convince your husband to attend afternoon calls, or at least make an appearance toward the end. Let us hope that all irritating men will run with their tails between their legs when they set eyes upon him."

Isabelle threw her head back and laughed. "Clearly, you're delusional, not that I blame you. If I had to listen to one more man wax poetic about your hair, I was going to grab the scissors and cut it all off."

"I would have allowed it."

"I know."

"Please?" Gwen was not against begging.

Isabelle sighed. "How do you imagine I could convince Dominique to do such a thing? He's still quite reclusive in society, and he despises socializing."

Gwen tilted her head to the side and patted her sister's hand. "Oh, I'm sure you can find a way to... convince him."

"Tart."

Gwen lifted her hands in innocence. "Says the one who's going to be convincing her husband all night long..."

"Gwen!" Isabelle scolded. "You shouldn't speak of such things!"

"We are sisters."

"You are unmarried," Isabelle pointed out, which truly just made Gwen feel worse, but she didn't want her sister to know she had unintentionally hurt her feelings. So she merely shrugged and gave a saucy grin. "Just because your reputation is less than pristine does not make this type of talk appropriate."

"I've had worse," Gwen said without thinking, then quickly rose from her seat to leave.

"Wait." Isabelle grabbed her hand. "You still haven't talked about what happened when you were gone those many months."

If Isabelle only knew the sacrifices Gwen had made for the family, sacrifices that made it so she gave away pieces of herself, of her pride, until she had nothing left. "It was nothing, dear, just an innocent adventure. Let us retire so I may ready myself for dinner. Apparently I'll be dining at your house."

"Hunter will be pleased."

"Hunter is easily pleased."

Isabelle lifted an eyebrow toward Gwen. "Are you sure there isn't more between the two of you? After all, he is an honorable man, though he does have his secrets."

Gwen sighed and felt her shoulders slump. "We all do."

Dinner progressed nicely, mainly because Hunter was nowhere to be seen, so Gwen was able to calmly enjoy a meal where she didn't have to fight off his seductive stares or cutting remarks. Which on one hand was nice; she did so enjoy dining with her sister and Dominique.

But her eyes kept glancing to the chair where Hunter had been sitting that morning. Suddenly overheated, she fanned herself and took a long drink of wine. Whatever was coming over her? Perhaps she was getting ill.

Her mind flashed to Hunter's seductive grin from that morning, and then his gentle touch this afternoon. She shouldn't have felt his warm hand through her skirts at all, but she had.

He had touched her, softly, when she came to his defense.

"Dear, are you well?" Isabelle asked.

"Of course." Gwen took another soothing drink of wine and watched as Dominique made lustful glances toward his wife. Now she truly felt like the third wheel.

"I have returned!" a loud voice announced from the doorway.

Gwen turned to see Hunter, cravat undone, a sort of substance down the front of his shirt, and swaying on his feet.

"Lovely." Dominique ignored Hunter and took a sip of wine. "I was wondering when the prodigal was to return. Got in another scuffle, did you?"

"With my horse." Hunter nodded and leaned against the wall, slowly sliding down it. Was no one going to help him?

He hit the floor with a thump.

Dominique took another sip of wine and kissed his wife's hand. "Shall we retire, my love?"

Isabelle sighed and rose from her chair. They walked arm in arm, taking special care to step over Hunter as they made their way from the room.

Had they forgotten about her?

"Oh, Gwen." Isabelle turned. "I'm so sorry. I don't know what came over me. I'm sorry, I forgot you were even sitting there."

Gwen knew exactly what had come over her sister. A very tall, dark, brooding, handsome prince wanted to have his way with her. She'd forget others existed if it were her in that position, as well.

"Never mind. I'll just call for the carriage and return

home."

Isabelle blushed and followed her husband up the stairs.

Ton families were rarely as blunt and familiar with one another. But most families hadn't been through what Gwen's had. So to see her sister giggle like a little girl as she went up the stairs with her husband didn't offend her. No, it just made her heart sad, for her sisters had found their matches.

And Gwen was alone with a drunk. The footmen had all but retired, and it was commonly known that Dominique only hired Russians, who were such independent sorts, it was a miracle they were around to help at all!

She grabbed her wine glass and walked over to Hunter, who had managed to fall asleep in a terribly uncomfortable position on the floor. His mouth was slightly ajar, leaving the perfect target for her attack.

First rule of spying. Never leave yourself exposed to the enemy. First rule of being the Wolf? Don't insult your partner repeatedly and expect her not to retaliate.

With a smirk, she poured a bit of wine down his front, only a section of it dribbling into his mouth. Red streaked down his chin. Curse the man, why the devil was he allowed to be so handsome when he was foxed?

He murmured something inaudible. She poured more wine.

His hand flew up and grabbed her arm. Quite fast for being so drunk.

"Having fun, my dear?" he purred into her ear, for he had pulled her down to the floor and nearly on his lap. His breath smelt nothing like whiskey; it was sweet, with a hint of wine and horse.

"Until you woke up, yes," she managed to grind out, even though his hand was burning through the skin on her neck.

"Wasn't sleeping," Hunter announced, nipping at her

ear. "Saints alive, what do you wash your skin with? It smells..." He inhaled again, his fingers lightly brushing the sensitive skin beneath her ear.

"Whatever it is..." She tried to jerk away. "At least I know that it attracts wolves."

"That it does." He chuckled, still not removing his hand. His fingers drummed against her pulse; she felt the rhythm of his touch all the way down to her toes as it hummed through her blood. "I like touching you."

"You're drunk."

His other hand moved to her waist, where he began sliding it across her stomach and down her hip toward her thigh. She hadn't the strength to move, his touch was such temptation, and she didn't know how to fight it.

His nose touched her neck as his lips moved across her bare skin. "Not that drunk."

"Yes, you are."

"I've had two glasses of whiskey. Believe me, I'm not drunk, but sometimes..." His lips moved to her jaw. "A person has to be what he is not, in order to gain information that he needs, yes?"

"Yes." She moaned. What was she saying yes to?

"And sometimes—" His teeth grazed her jaw. "A man has to do things he'd rather not do, for the sake of his country, yes?"

What did he say? Something about living in the country? Men in the country? His fingers moved from her neck and slid down to the front of her dress. "Yes?"

"Oftentimes..." Why was he still talking? "It is imperative to be reminded that you are not yourself when you are owned by the Crown. And even when you want something so badly you can taste it..." His tongue traced her lower lip. "You must say no."

"Yes."

"Say no." Hunter moaned against her lips.

"Why?"

"Because I'm drunk and about to take advantage of you."

"You said you weren't drunk."

"I feel drunk right now." He kissed her hard across the mouth and all she could think was, *Me too, me too.*

CHAPTER FOURTEEN

Red—

Forgive me if I am wrong, but did you just first encourage me to bite and then act on instinct, and finally refer to you? My dear! A worthy opponent you are, but do you truly think it safe for your virtue to make advances toward an animal such as me? You've done nothing but encourage the beast within, and I guarantee you that soon, you will see why they call me the Wolf of Haverstone. By the by, did you get my drawing? I worked hard on that. Sheep are not the easiest of God's creatures to draw. Tell me, my dear, do you like being compared to a farm animal? Or would you rather be compared to a tiger? Spend the night in my bed and let me decide. Woof.

—Wolf

BLASTED CONSCIENCE. WHY WAS he suddenly developing one, now of all times? When he had the most beautiful woman in his arms moaning and rubbing against him?

He sighed. "I have something for you." That came out wrong. He tried again. "A surprise."

Gwen stiffened in his arms.

He should have let his horse finish him off, for he truly had fallen off of it. Not that it was his own fault. Someone had shot at him.

But that was beside the point.

"Shall I start over?"

"That would be best," Gwen said.

"First, help me off the floor."

Gwen pushed herself away from him and onto her feet. "Why are you on the floor to begin with, if you are not even that drunk?"

"Attention." He chuckled. "Not but a few months ago, Dominique was shot in the arm. Nearly died. I wanted to see what it was like to be nursed to health by a fallen angel."

Gwen rolled her eyes. "Who says I'm fallen?"

"All you need to do is ask, and I'll do the pushing."

"Must everything be a joke to you?"

Hunter sighed. "If I cannot joke, then I must settle with reality, which frankly makes me wish my horse would have finished me off."

Gwen said nothing as he shrugged and staggered to his feet. He probably should not have said that aloud and was momentarily thankful that she chose not to comment. He stumbled a bit and swore.

Gwen cursed and put an arm around him, then gasped. "Hunter, you've been shot."

"Oh, now I remember!" He snapped his fingers. "Yes, that was what I was going to tell you." He looked up into her crystal blue eyes and grinned. Most likely from the alcohol, not the simple fact that she had her arms around him, and he'd just finished kissing her. "I've been shot."

"Yes. I can see that."

"But I didn't feel a thing. Remarkable!"

"Thus the drinking?"

Hunter suddenly felt faint. "Well, yes, I didn't feel a thing immediately, that is, until I tried to get back on my horse and that's when I began to wail like an adolescent girl."

"Never been shot before, hmm?" Gwen asked.

"No." Hunter took a steadying breath. Sweat poured down his face. "Never been kicked by a horse before, either. An entirely uninteresting experience I have no desire to repeat."

Gwen stopped walking. Why had she stopped? Did she not see that he was clearly bleeding all over the place?

"Your horse kicked you as well?"

"Yes." He gritted his teeth. "But to be fair, he's never been shot at, either. Easy mistake."

Gwen said something about the stupidity of beasts and wolves, or perhaps she said wolves were just as stupid as beasts. Whatever she said, he had trouble hearing, since he was going in and out of consciousness. It did not help that his vision was suddenly going very, very dark.

He cringed as she helped him walk. He decided the only way he was going to make it any farther was to keep himself awake and distracted. "I had two drinks at White's earlier this afternoon and emptied the contents of my flask on the way here to numb the pain, though I think your mouth helped more than the whiskey. Care to give it another try?"

"That depends." Gwen sighed. "Are you feeling the need to get shot again?"

Hunter waved into the air. "Take me to Dominique's study. We will have to dress the wound."

"We?"

"Yes." He cursed aloud.

"As in you and I?"

"Is there anyone else here?"

Servants walked silently by them, for the most part. The odd Russian butler ignored everyone anyway. Besides, he could not call for a doctor. He didn't want anyone knowing that his life was in danger. That would just draw more attention to Gwen, and the last thing he wanted was her in the line of fire.

"I cannot simply…" Gwen waved her free hand in the air as she braced him against her side. "Sew up your wound!"

Hunter leaned against her even more heavily than before. "But I thought you were a woman?"

"Pardon?" A perfectly arched brow lifted, as if to taunt him into thinking she was upset. Surely she knew her place in the world.

Hunter chuckled, partly because he was somewhat foxed and near fainting, and partly because he found her angry eyebrow intriguing. All dark and menacing, as if it had all the power in the world to make him feel intimidated. "Women, they sew all day long. They gossip, they sew, they drink tea, and they gossip some more. Surely you know how to do some of those things?"

Gwen was silent.

She helped him the rest of the way into the study and promptly dropped him onto the floor — onto his wound, to be more precise, and though the bullet had gone clean through his side, it hurt like the devil.

"What was that for?" he roared, suddenly seeing two of her standing before him.

"You son of a—"

"Sheep! Sheep! Bahhhh!"

"Are you mad? What nonsense are you spouting?" Gwen knelt by his side, concern etched in her brow as she pressed a hand against his forehead.

Hmm, that felt good. "Sheep," he repeated. Perhaps pretending to be mad with fever had its advantages.

"Sheep," she agreed. "Why are you screaming about sheep? Why are you making sheep noises? Oh, I've gone mad. Why do I even ask you these things when I know you're going to somehow turn it into something sensual or erotic?"

"I hate to break it to you, my dear, but there is nothing erotic about a sheep."

Gwen smacked him across the shoulder.

Hunter winced. "Sorry, I was just trying to keep you from screaming at me, causing Dominique and Isabelle to stop dallying upstairs and the servants to come running. We are spies, you know. Show a little decorum."

Hunter could have sworn that, in that moment, he saw her eyes flash pure murder, as if she dreamt she could have a pistol and shoot him repeatedly with it, or perhaps knock him upside the head with her hand or a blunt object, or perhaps throw him off his horse or— "Ohh..." He moaned. "I cannot decide what hurts worse, the bullet or my backside."

"Finally turned into a horse's a—"

Hunter clamped his hand over her mouth. "Whiskey, towels, and please cease your cursing before I'm forced to cover that dirty and delicious mouth with my lips again."

Gwen jerked away and went to the sideboard. She loudly pulled out two glasses and poured the whiskey, sloshing it over the side.

He muttered his thanks as she returned, only when he held out his hand for the glass, she lifted it to her own lips and drank heavily. "I believe you've had enough. This is for me. I know nothing of wounds, and I fear I may be a hindrance."

Hunter grimaced as pain shot down his side again. Gwen left the room and quickly returned with a cloth. "This will have to do."

"It is dirty." Hunter stared at the revolting cloth. What did she do? Stomp on it before bringing it in here? Feed it to his horse? Allow a chicken to relieve itself on the threads?

Gwen huffed and sat down. "It is fine. Besides, it is only to catch the whiskey after I pour it across the wound."

"Do you know?" Hunter felt the sweat drop from his

chin. "I'm feeling much better. I—"

"Be still." Gwen was already lifting up his shirt. That was nice. Perhaps if he closed his eyes, he could imagine that she was seducing him. Her cold hands felt like heaven against his hot skin. He sighed loudly and then moaned.

Gwen gasped. He opened his eyes. "What?"

"There is a lot of blood." Her face went white as a sheet.

"Red," Hunter urged, not sure why he was using her little pet name. "Sweetheart, it must be cleaned. Besides, I'm a wolf. We are tolerant of flesh wounds."

"Are you now?" Her lower lip trembled before her teeth bit down on it and chewed. Oh, what he wouldn't give to be that lip instead of a wolf. Perhaps he should change his name. Yes, Gwen's lip, sounded much more fierce.

Obviously he was more foxed than he'd realized, considering he was contemplating changing his nickname to something so absurd. But blast, how she had plump lips.

"This is going to hurt." She tilted the glass of whiskey.

"Already does," he grumbled, as the first remnants of alcohol washed over his wound. He clenched his teeth. He would not scream, not in front of Gwen. Distraction. He needed a distraction.

He felt the sweat pour down his neck as she began to pour more whiskey. All the while Hunter focused on nothing but her eyes.

And then she looked at him.

A *moment* is what the storybooks would call it. Time did indeed seem to stand still, but it could have been his inability to think straight. All he knew in that moment was that it was probable he was developing perhaps a small attachment to the woman.

Not an "Allow me to begin naming our future children" type of attraction; more of one that perhaps a fellow feels deep in his soul when he sees a type of loneliness in someone else's eyes and realizes he could be the one to take it away.

"Sleep with me," he blurted.

Gwen's mouth dropped open. Carefully, she placed the glass on the floor and used her dress to press against the wound.

Hunter's breath came in short gasps. "Blast, woman! Must you be so rough?"

Gwen turned a brilliant shade of crimson. "I bet you say those sweet words to all the ladies."

Too shocked that the minx hadn't backed away or slapped him, but fired back with her own innuendo, Hunter promptly passed out.

CHAPTER FIFTEEN

Wolf—

Better to be compared to a sheep than become a wolf's prey. Apologies, but the minute I saw the picture I quickly threw it into the fire. It frightened me, you see. I was under the impression it was a self-portrait and you know how I feel about you being anywhere in my bedroom, real or not.

—Red

GWEN TAPPED HUNTER'S SHOULDER.

Had she killed him?

She pushed him a bit.

He moaned.

Should she retrieve the smelling salts? Did men need smelling salts? She whispered into his ear, "Hunter, are you able to hear me?"

Motionless. She snapped out of her panic and ran to the sideboard and poured some more whiskey into the glass. When the rim was near spilling over, she brought it over to Hunter and threw it in his face.

"What the—" Hunter jerked out of his state. Whiskey droplets fell from his chin. He blinked, once, twice, and then shook his head. "Am I not foxed enough that you felt the need for me to bathe in whiskey?"

"I thought you died."

"So you were burying me in my sin, is that it?"

Gwen swallowed. "I- I didn't know what else to do."

"Yes, well, apparently whiskey is the answer to everything, or so good Englishmen say. Now help me up. I must somehow make it up the stairs and into my room, where I can properly bandage myself without passing out again."

"You mean fainting?"

"Men do *not* faint." Hunter struggled to get to his feet. "We merely close our eyes for a spell."

"You were unconscious."

"I was dreaming of a beautiful woman…"

Gwen rolled her eyes and helped him up.

"…she was wearing red. And she confessed her love to me not once, not twice, but thrice!"

"Interesting."

"My story?" Hunter held tightly onto her as she led him down the hall and slowly up the stairs.

"No." Blast, but the man was heavy. "The fact that alcohol could so easily be soaked in through the skin that you would start to hallucinate."

"Hmmph," Hunter grumbled, as they made their way up to the second level and slowly stumbled down the hall.

They walked the rest of the way in silence. Hunter winced as Gwen used her free hand to push the door open. Once they were inside, Gwen gently laid him onto the bed, not because she wanted to but because she figured if she went about it more aggressively he would get the wrong sort of idea.

Even though the idea of being alone with him in his room

was causing her treacherous body to heat. No self-respecting woman should be alone with a man, especially not one whose reputation hung in the balance.

Hunter groaned and pointed toward a small dresser. "Inside the first drawer is enough supplies to pack the wound. If you would be so kind."

He laid back across the bed.

Gwen briskly walked to the dresser and pulled open the first drawer, then she really wished she wouldn't have.

"How many knives do you possess?" Knives of every sort littered the inside of the first drawer. Did the man actually use them with his victims or have a strange fascination?

"Under the knives," Hunter said, ignoring her question. "Look under the knives."

She lifted the board where the knives lay. It clicked open and then pulled back, as if it was on some sort of mechanical device. "Fascinating."

"Yes, perhaps we can discuss my many treasures before I bleed to death. Once I've closed my eyes, you may touch as many knives as you want, including mine."

Gwen felt herself blush but ignored him. Was everything a joke to this man? Every blasted little thing? She quickly grabbed the bandages and marched over to him. He leaned up on his elbows. Sweat still marked his brow. With a curse, Hunter got to a sitting position and attempted pulling off his jacket. But once he raised his arms, he cursed a blue streak and paused. "A little help, please."

The sooner she helped him, the sooner she could go home. Gwen licked her lips and began tugging at the jacket. She tried, she really tried to keep her eyes framed onto his jacket as she helped him tug out of it. But the minute she removed it, she was faced with his shirtsleeves.

Gulping, she helped pull that off of him and told her hands to stop shaking. The situation seemed too intimate; it felt too intimate, as if they were about to share the same bed. Hah, if she ever shared his bed, it would be a product of lust and nothing more. The man had no heart, and even if he did, she highly doubted he would share it with a virgin.

"My thanks," Hunter breathed as he placed the bandage on his side. Her eyes trailed down his muscular stomach. It seemed the Wolf liked to box or play, or do whatever wolves did out in the wilderness.

Her eyes flickered down as Hunter finished bandaging himself. "Now." He winced, commanding her attention. She looked into his eyes. "I think it's safe to say I'm in danger."

"Your powers of deduction astound me." Gwen swallowed and fought to keep her eyes on his, though it was one of the most difficult things she'd never tried, for the man was beautiful. It shouldn't be allowed for a man to have such smooth skin. Tight muscles rippled across his stomach and chest. His skin wasn't pale like that of most Englishmen. No, it was the perfect color, almost bronzed, as if he spent a great deal of time out of his clothes, which honestly made a lot of sense.

"The people of London believe me to be retired. There is no reason I would be an open threat. The traitor has to be one of those three men. I do not think the person shooting at me aimed to kill. It was more of a warning than anything. It's possible what you said during their visits struck a nerve." He winced and continued. "Gwen, you need to find out who the mole is. When you go on your walks and dally in the carriage, have a care. You are not debuting in order to win a husband. You have a job to do."

"Are you scolding me?" *And drunk? Unbelievable!*

"No." Hunter reached out and grasped her hand. "I'm merely telling you the truth. You must be careful. After your carriage ride with Trehmont, find a way to meet me so we can discuss any information you may find. Talk with him about the French, see if he gets nervous, study his mannerisms, is he always looking at his pocket watch? Does he seem to defer your questions at all? You know what I mean." He leaned up and winked. "Where shall we meet?"

"The masquerade." Gwen nodded. "Nobody will recognize us."

Hunter groaned. "Please tell me you're not referring to Madame LaMont's masquerade?"

"It will not be so bad."

"I will want to shoot myself the minute I arrive, but yes, if you say it won't be so bad, I'll take your word for it."

Gwen let out a heavy sigh. "I'll be dressed as a shepherdess."

"Not a sheep?" Hunter grinned. Blast, how she hated that grin. His glaring white teeth irritated her. Was everything perfect about him? Without thinking, she looked down at his body again. Yes. It seemed everything was perfect. Stupid man.

"No, I thought it unsafe, considering the circumstances."

"Circumstances?" Hunter narrowed his eyes. "Whatever do you mean?"

Gwen began walking toward the door, then turned and gave him a wink. "I have it on good authority a wolf is to make an appearance. Wouldn't want to tempt him, now, would I?"

"You tempt him by breathing," Hunter whispered.

"Is that your way of telling me to stop breathing?"

"No." Hunter's eyes narrowed. He looked away and began to slouch against the bed. "Not at all. Gwen, be careful, please. I—" He looked away and cursed. "I cannot lose you. Do you understand?"

Confused by the sudden hurt she saw in his eyes, she nodded and gave him, the great Wolf, a curtsy. "I will be safe. I promise."

"Thank you."

"Goodnight, Hunter."

"Goodnight, my little Red..." His eyes slowly closed as his body fell against the bed.

Gwen quietly stepped out into the hall and made her way down the stairs, hoping and praying that her footman had had enough good sense to hide her carriage once the hour grew late.

Thankfully, when she came around the house, she noticed him sitting near the back of the servants' entrance.

"Home, please," she announced. He nodded and offered his arm.

"I took the liberty of taking the carriage home and walking here myself when the hour grew late, my lady. I hope you do not mind, but I will escort you on the short walk to your sister's residence."

William had been in the service of their family for nearly a decade. He was also one of the many servants who kept her secret. She paid him well for his silence, but even if she didn't, he would still be loyal. For he had loved her father, and she knew that he wanted to protect her.

They walked home in silence. Gwen would never admit to Hunter that she was frightened, but she was. Whoever had shot at him had been trying to kill him, and she had no doubt in her mind that one of those men had to be the three they were suspicious of. She just needed to find out whom, and fast.

CHAPTER SIXTEEN

Red—

Tsk, tsk, tsk, you should know better by now. Any time you use the word bedroom, I take it as an invitation.

—Wolf

HUNTER GRIMACED AS HE looked at the large structure in front of him. The house was monstrous Truly, it would have been better for the old duke to make a flag with his name sewn across it than build such a monstrosity that the whole of London could see his house from miles away.

But that was how the old Duke of Lainhart wanted it. Grumpy old man. Hunter paced in front of the gate for ten minutes before pulling out his flask and taking a sip of brandy.

He never drank in the mornings.

Since when had he resorted to drinking when he was to face the old man? He needed to face him sooner or later, especially considering Wilkins had just that morning sent him a note stating it was imperative he ask Lainhart about the three gentlemen they were investigating, considering at one point they had all worked for him.

If Lainhart still possessed all his sensibilities and was not half the man he used to be, he would be the best the War Office had as far as codes were concerened. It seemed that all the French did was try to break the codes of the English in hopes to discover where troops were stationed or how many English were truly hurt in the war. With the war looming like a dark cloud over all of England, it was a sure tragedy that one of their own was not only breaking the codes but gaining a profit from treason. Hunter sighed heavily and pulled out his pocket watch. It was still early. But then again, he was never late. He had dallied for as long as he could.

He walked slowly up the stairs and grasped the cold knocker between his fingers. Suddenly he was transported back to when he had first come to call.

"Hunter!" Lucy ran out of the house and into his arms. Much to the dismay of her parents and their stern butler. She always made a spectacle of herself.

"My love." Hunter grinned and set her on her feet. "I have come to call, as you demanded at last night's ball."

"Rogue." She swatted him. "I did not demand; I merely asked if you would be happening by during the visiting hours."

"That you did." He grinned and kissed her hand. So began their quick courtship.

He shivered beneath the wet air and waited for the butler to answer.

Nothing.

He knocked again.

Finally, after an eternity, the door opened just slightly. "Yes?"

"Haverstone to see Lainhairt." This was always how it had been. Lucy's grandfather despised him and still blamed him for his favorite granddaughter's death. It did not help matters that both her parents had passed a short time after his and Lucy's marriage as well. Leaving Lucy and Eastbrook as the only two remaining relatives.

And now, it was just Eastbrook.

"Haverstone, you say?" the scratchy voice said from the other side of the door.

"Live and in the flesh."

A snort was heard from the other end. "The duke is ill and not receiving callers."

"He will receive me." Hunter pushed the door open. "Now."

He'd expected the usual butler. But the man looking at him was anything but the pristine butler who had worked for their family for years.

"Who are you?"

The man shrugged. Hair covered his entire face. His hair, the same color as Hunter's, hung down to his shoulders. A patch covered his eye, and he walked with a limp.

"I'm speaking to you," Hunter said crisply.

"I realize that," the man said. "But I imagine you like to hear yourself speak often. Therefore I will let you speak and give you the idea that I am listening, rather than counting down the minutes until you exit this house."

"How dare you speak to me that way. Do you not know who I am?"

"Oh." The man turned, this time glaring at Hunter. "I know exactly who you are, and it makes me sick. To think that poor Lucy's memory is tainted by…"

Hunter lunged for the man. "Never speak of her!"

The butler backed up and laughed. "Always the same. Fighting and reacting. The Duke is upstairs in his usual room. And when you speak, do yourself a favor: think beforehand."

The man hobbled off, leaving Hunter angrier than he'd been in months. How dare he speak to him in such a way! He knew nothing!

Cursing, he stomped up the stairs and threw open the doors to his grandfather's rooms.

The smell of medicine burned his nostrils. Shaking, he slowly walked to the bed where the Duke of Lainhart was laying.

"C-came," the old duke blurted. His glassy eyes held unshed tears as he pointed his finger into the air.

"Oh." A maid appeared at the old Duke's side. "Pardon me, your grace. I did not hear anyone enter into the room. I'll just leave you alone now."

She looked vaguely familiar. Then again, everything in this house seemed familiar to Hunter. He nodded in her direction as she exited, then called, "Wait, what is he saying?"

Lainhart had one finger pointed in the air while his other hand hastily wrote across a piece of blackboard.

The maid smiled warmly. "When he points one finger into the air, it either means *yes* or *wait*. When he turns his thumb down, it means *no* or that he disapproves."

"Right."

The maid disappeared and Hunter returned his attention to Lainhart. His finger was still thrust in the air while he concentrated on the board he was shakily writing across.

Nothing better than being disapproved of in more than one language. Now he would have to suffer knowing that Lainhart disapproved of him in English, sign language, and of course, the written word.

Lainhart grunted and looked up, his gray hair falling near his chin. The man had always been like a giant to Hunter. Where muscles protruded, a nightshirt pooled around the man's waist. His face was tired; deep lines of exhaustion created a map of age across the man's face. His eyebrows drew in as he turned the blackboard toward Hunter and pointed.

"Disappointed."

"Me, too," Hunter agreed. "Though I imagine we are

disappointed for two entirely different things. There is, er, something that needs your attention. As you know, I still work for the War Office. It seems that some of the codes you created are being broken and given to the French."

Lainhart shook his head violently and pointed down.

"Right. I do not have the capability to understand the codes and the three men who are suspected are ones who worked directly under you. Before you retired, was there any one of them you suspected?"

Lainhart closed his eyes and pointed up then very slowly wrote on the chalkboard. "All."

Hunter cursed. "All of them? You suspected all of them?"

Lainhart nodded.

"Why haven't you gone to anyone? Why haven't you said anything?"

His grandfather drew a line through the word and wrote again. "Need more evidence."

Hunter sighed. "I will find more evidence. You can count on that."

Lainhart leaned forward and coughed. Hunter held him so he wouldn't fall from the bed, but the minute he touched him, Lainhart stopped coughing. His knobby hands pulled at Hunter's jacket, and then he turned his head slightly to the nightstand and gave a firm nod and released him.

Hunter reached into the nightstand and pulled out a thick envelope. Evidence, it had to be. If anything, it would at least help Hunter find whom his own grandfather suspected the most.

The old man shook his head and pointed his finger up into the air. Hunter waited patiently while Lainhart drew a line through the word and wrote again.

This time it did not take long. He held up the board and pointed to the phrase, "Find killer."

Hunter felt the blood drain from his face. "What killer?

Of whom are you speaking?" Were they not just talking about codes a few minutes ago?

"L-l-lucy," Lainhart ground out, his speech slurred. Sweat poured down his face as he shook his head back and forth. A tear escaped his eye. "F-f-f-inddd."

So Lainhart had gone mad. "It was an accident. She was not murdered."

Lainhart began yelling and thrashing his head back and forth. "N-n-no!"

The door to the room burst open. The old butler hobbled in and began yelling. "Is your plan to kill him, then? His heart is too weak! Leave at once!"

Hunter didn't need to be told twice. His heart twisted in his chest. How he wished that Lainhart was right, for if Lucy had been killed, that meant Hunter could do something about it now, which he couldn't.

He nodded to the butler, and made his way down the hall and down the stairs. It wasn't until he'd almost reached the door that he remembered he'd left the large packet on Lainhart's bed. Quickly, he turned, and cursed. The butler stood just behind him.

"His grace wanted you to have this. Please, do not return until you have good news."

It was possible the whiskey was talking, but the butler's one eye seemed to penetrate through Hunter's soul. Strange, his eyes were familiar. Hunter leaned forward to examine the man's face further.

"My interests lie with women, I assure you." The butler grunted and thumped Hunter on the back before leading him toward the door.

"I wasn't, that is to say, I was just examining your face to see—" Hunter scratched his head. "What did you say your name was?"

The butler gently pushed Hunter out onto the step. "I

didn't. Now have a good day."

CHAPTER SEVENTEEN

Wolf—

Then allow me to make myself clear. If you were in my bedroom (and yes, I dare say bedroom again; careful not to drool) I would most likely mistake you for a hairy intruder and shoot you on the spot. Though have a care, I do not wish to see blood on my floor. Perhaps then I would just push you out the window and allow the ground to break your fall. Wolves always land on their feet. Or wait, am I getting you confused with a more intelligent species?

—Red

GWEN TRIED DESPERATELY TO seem interested when Trehmont began discussing his desire to set himself apart as a gentleman of fashion.

"For you see, French blood runs alive and true through these sturdy veins of mine. Class and fashion are in my blood, much like passion. Tell me, my dear, have you ever been with a Frenchman?" He waggled his eyebrows and laughed, though to be fair, his laugh was more of a gurgle. Apparently having a perpetual cold was another one of the things that luckily ran through his sturdy veins.

Gwen folded her hands tightly and tried desperately to keep herself from screaming at the infuriating man. She was here to do a job. If she must flirt in order to gain information, then at least she could know that after this horrid carriage ride, she would be able to plunge into a bath and wash the filth of this encounter away.

"I do not believe that topic is appropriate for an afternoon ride, my lord." She patted his hand, careful not to jerk back when he grasped it between his clammy fingers.

"Ah, but I forget, you are pure." The way he said *pure* made her very much doubt his intentions. Would she never be viewed as such?

Trehmont pulled back on the reins and stopped the curricle. "Shall we walk for a spell?"

Perhaps she could spook the horses in hopes that he would be more concerned for his curricle than her?

He offered his hand. Why the devil wasn't he wearing gloves anyway? She could practically feel the sweat from his hand seep into her kid gloves. Disgusting.

"Now, where were we?" Trehmont made a grand show of laughing, as if the topic of their previous conversation had been amusing or interesting. Unfortunately Hyde Park was anything but vacant. It seemed every fashionable soul was out and about, wanting to be seen.

Just her luck, she was to be seen with the slimiest of them all.

"Trehmont, do tell me, has this war been difficult for you? All things considering?"

Trehmont gritted his teeth and looked away from her. "I am not sure I gain your meaning, my lady?"

"You're half French," she stated rather boldly.

He stopped in his tracks and after several seconds of staring at the grass looked up to meet her gaze. "My lady, the

142

only French traits I possess are those of style and passion, I assure you."

Which truly wasn't all that assuring, considering his present style. A blue waistcoat with yellow buttons was offset with a wildly tied orange cravat.

And if his clothing wasn't hint enough, when he said *passion* and smiled, she noticed a piece of cabbage stuck in his teeth.

Right. If he was innocent, Hunter was a virgin.

"Now, where were we?" Trehmont tucked her arm under his and patted it, as if she were a child he had just put in her place.

"We were discussing your French blood. I am so relieved, my lord, that you are not the type to align yourself with the French while living in the country fighting for your freedom." If he was guilty, he would at least flinch beneath her statement.

"But of course," Trehmont said smoothly. "I do owe England everything. Besides, my mother was English."

"Interesting. I—"

"Lady Gwendolyn, fancy seeing you here." Hunter strolled up to them with a grim expression on his face. His eyes flickered to Trehmont's hand on Gwen's; if possible, his expression darkened even more.

"Is it, though?" Gwen said through clenched teeth.

"Is what?" Hunter's eyes were still trained on Trehmont's hand.

"Fancy?"

"Whose fancy?" Hunter's head snapped up.

Gwen made it a point to glare at him. Perhaps he could read her body language and know he was not welcome.

"Might I join you two for a walk?"

Or not.

"Of course," Trehmont answered as he pulled Gwen

closer to his side.

Hunter, clearly not getting the hint, fell into step beside them. "By the by, Trehmont, you will never guess what I heard on my way over here."

"Hmm." Trehmont nodded to a passing couple. "And what is that?"

"You own a small estate outside of Bath, do you not?"

Trehmont scowled. "Not that it is any business of yours, but I own several properties, as I said the day before." This he directed at Gwen. "Rumors of my ruin are grossly exaggerated. I do quite well."

"Oh, dear." Hunter stopped walking. "Then perhaps you should sit for a spell."

"Sit?" Trehmont looked at Hunter as if he were going mad. "Why the devil would I sit?"

"Your property. It seems there has been a fire, and well…" Hunter pulled out a handkerchief and wiped beneath his eyes. "Everything is lost."

Trehmont paled. "Everything, you say?"

Hunter nodded. "Everything. But never fear! For you said so yourself. You have plenty of property! Come into money, have you?"

Trehmont cursed a blue streak, threw his beaver hat to the ground, and began stomping wildly around it.

Gwen leaned in toward Hunter. "Does he believe his hat is on fire, as well?"

Trehmont yelled again and stomped, cursing as he did so.

"Perhaps he's finally gone mad," Hunter observed quietly.

"All of my…" Trehmont paused.

"Possessions?" Hunter offered. "You mean possessions, do you not? But why, if you have so much property, would you choose to store all your valuables at such a location?"

Trehmont's face turned red. "I do not answer to you! Good day!"

"They will kill him in prison." Hunter sighed and looked at the poor beaver hat. "Silly, but I feel sorrier for the hat."

"Prison?" Gwen nearly shouted.

"Hats are too beautiful not to have feelings, don't you agree, Red? I'd expect you to slap me if I ever treated my things in such a fashion."

"Prison?" Gwen said again, this time nearer to Hunter's ear. Clearly he was having trouble hearing.

"Hats are quite expensive. Did you know that just last week, when I was on my way to Hoby's to buy some new boots, I—"

"Hunter!" Gwen grabbed his arm and pinched. "What the devil is wrong with you? Stop spouting nonsense about hats. Why is Trehmont going to prison?"

"Oh. That." Hunter smiled and jerked his arm away, careful to smooth down the nonexistent wrinkles on his perfect jacket. "Seems the man has been smuggling for the past few years. But what I find interesting is that the War Office has known all along. They've used his smuggling business as a front to transfer messages back and forth during the war. Seems the money wasn't enough for Trehmont, and he started his own side business. I do wonder what the War Office will think of that."

"Smuggling?"

"Yes. And gaining quite a profit."

"How did you know?"

"I read minds," Hunter stated dryly.

"Can you read mine now?" Gwen purposefully thought of pushing Hunter into the river.

"Death." He choked and then laughed. "See, I told you I could read minds."

"Aghh!" Gwen stomped her foot and lunged for him.

He pulled her into a tight embrace and whispered in her ear, "Have a care, my dear, we are in public and we cannot look too familiar."

"Then release me."

Hunter sighed but did not relinquish his grip. "If I release you now, it will look like a lover's quarrel."

"What differences does now or five minutes make?"

Hunter whispered into her ear, his breath tickling the delicate flesh around her neck. "A lover's embrace, my dear. It must look like we are engaging in something forbidden."

"I am ruined already. The only men who are interested are ones who smuggle and apparently keep food saved in their teeth."

"Not all of them, Gwen." Hunter's voice was gruff as he released her and set her to rights. "Not all of them."

He offered his arm. She took it, nearly forgetting that her maid had been following them the entire time. She motioned for her to continue behind them and allowed Hunter to lead her away from Trehmont's discarded hat.

"How did you find out about the smuggling?"

"I read."

"Good for you." She scowled.

He chuckled. "My grandfather has been collecting evidence against our three suspects for quite some time. I was reading through his notes this afternoon and came upon the smuggling bit, wanted to have a bit of fun with Trehmont and see how he reacted."

Gwen stopped and laughed. "The grandfather who hates you?"

Hunter growled. "Yes. From hence forward, let us refer to him as the one who hates me. Makes one feel so valued."

"Sorry." Gwen nodded to another passing couple. "What else did the evidence say?"

"Apparently, Lainhart has been doing some research of

RACHEL VAN DYKEN

his own. He's been having Wilkins, Trehmont, Redding, and Hollins followed for the past ten years."

"But why? And why has it been recorded? And why Wilkins?"

"That, my dear, I believe I can answer. Lainhart invented many of the codes used for the ciphers."

"So?"

Hunter looked down at the ground, his shoulders slumped. "So, my dear, the only men in the world who know how to decipher the codes — the only men privy to that information — are the ones we are investigating. Surely Wilkins told you this?"

"Th-the mole." Gwen paced in front of him. "The mole is one of the three and has been leaking top secret information to the French? Locations of units, battle plans... Am I right?"

"Whoever said sheep weren't intelligent?"

"Funny, I thought I was a nut?"

"Oh, silly me. I had forgotten already." Hunter winked. "And yes, you are correct in your assumptions. It is imperative that we discover who is selling this information."

Gwen chewed her lip and nodded. It truly was up to her to discover which of the men were deciphering the codes for the French. The only way to figure it out was to either break into their homes or follow them. There was of course seduction. Many a man would tell secrets for sex, wouldn't they? But was she truly willing to give that part of herself for the greater good?

Her thoughts troubled her as Hunter led her to his ducal carriage.

"Tonight, we shall discuss matters in earnest, where we will not be watched. I will, of course, make my return debut at the masquerade, sweep you off your feet, and take you into a darkened corner as is my custom. And you will, of course, sigh longingly into my chest, and people will assume I am trying to

147

seduce you. It will be the perfect ploy so we may talk." He chuckled as if what he was saying wasn't ridiculous and as if the entire world wasn't crashing down around them. Why did everything have to be laced with sarcasm? Could he never be real? And if he lacked the ability to truly be himself, how could she ever trust him?

The carriage stopped in front of her house.

"Mary, you may go inside and see to having a pot of tea ready for when I return. It seems his grace and I have a few things to discuss." She waited for her maid to exit the carriage and turned her full attention to Hunter. "So that is all?" Gwen said. "You refuse to explain to me what will happen to Trehmont? Why you finally decided to visit your grandfather after all these years?"

Hunter's lips parted revealing a shy smile. "Apologies, you lost me when you mentioned Trehmont. Suffice to say, all I could think about was that silly hat. It shall get rained on, no doubt about it."

"Hunter!" Gwen raised her voice. "Be serious for once in your life."

He moved so fast she didn't have time to brace herself as he gripped her arm and pulled her against him. "You know nothing about my life."

Gwen trembled beneath his touch. "I know more than you think."

"Enlighten me." His teeth clenched; the muscles in his face tensed as if they too were holding their breath.

"You aren't as stupid as you appear."

"Bravo. It seems you just paid me a compliment, however passive-aggressive it may have been."

He swallowed and pulled back but Gwen wasn't ready for the conversation to be over with. "How can I trust you, really trust you, when you hide behind a mask, even with me."

"I have no idea what you are referring to." He looked away, a smirk on his lips. "Kindly exit the carriage, I have an appointment."

"Not until you tell me why."

"Why?"

"Why are you like this? What happened to you?"

Hunter cursed and looked down at his hands. "I was late."

Gwen waited for him to elaborate and when he didn't, she was at a loss for how to respond.

"Go." Hunter's voice trembled. "I shall see you tonight."

Confused, Gwen did as he said, but vowed to herself that she would find out what he tried so hard to hide from. Being late? The answer made no sense whatsoever. But then again, Hunter rarely made sense.

Tonight. Tonight she would use everything she'd learned as a spy to find out his secret.

Why was it that when she thought of seducing the Wolf, warmth spread through her body? Perhaps he was a risk worth taking; perhaps with him, she could give that part of herself. For regardless of how he saw himself, to her he was not only a worthy opponent, but the type of man worth fighting for.

CHAPTER EIGHTEEN

Red—

Wolves are by nature very intelligent creatures. Take for example the fact that they are feared amongst humans and beasts alike! My dear, if as a wolf, I do not cause you to tremble with that same fear, perhaps you will tremble with something else entirely when our partnership is through. One can only hope, and you, my dear, give me great cause to hope.

—Wolf

AFTER HIS EXCHANGE WITH Gwen, Hunter immediately went to Wilkins' residence. The house looked dead as usual, dead except for the fact that Hollins was exiting in a hurry, a note clenched in his hand.

It would have seemed normal, but it was not the correct day for any sort of code to be transferred; that is, not unless it was an emergency, and they were losing horribly, and Hunter would have been the first to know that.

Leaving his carriage, he followed Hollins down the street. After a few blocks or so, Hollins took a turn and disappeared.

Fantastic.

He searched the area for a while but found nothing. With a curse, he walked back to the house and knocked.

Wilkins himself answered. "Hunter, my boy, how is the investigation? Did you need something?"

Wilkins' demeanor was so vastly different than before that at first Hunter thought he was foxed. "Er, yes, I was going to continue my investigation and the trail has lead me to Hollins. Have you seen him recently?"

With a laugh, Wilkins shook his head. "No. It is very rare for me to see Hollins when there are no codes scheduled for transfer."

"That is what I thought. Well, thank you."

Hunter walked back to his carriage more confused than he'd been in a while. Wilkins was clearly lying, Hollins was delivering notes on the wrong day, and he still had to go to a blasted masquerade that evening!

Hunter waited in the shadows. True to his word, he'd dressed as a wolf. Donning all black was not stretching his current style too much, but wearing a cape truly did have its advantages. It was covered in fur and made him feel like an oversized rug. He also had a sneaking suspicion that, if he stood near the wall that was currently painted a ghastly brown color, he blended in quite well.

His eyes greedily searched for Gwen.

Hah! Gwen. The same woman who caused him so much emotional turmoil, he had nearly run his horse into a tree during his afternoon ride. After their discussion in the carriage, he wanted nothing more than to take the first ship out of port and find himself in a foreign country.

She could not get too close.

He would not allow it.

Everything he touched seemed to wither away and die. And everyone he ever loved left him.

Trusting a woman was akin to inviting death into his life again, and though he hadn't a care for his own soul, he would not stand by and be responsible for Gwen losing hers.

He circled the ballroom twice.

Had his cape caught underneath at least four different slippers, all belonging to females who looked as if they wanted to devour him.

And drank two glasses of wine.

All before he found her.

Had he been holding anything, he would have dropped it.

Trouble. Her entire costume bespoke trouble. If that costume was true to a shepherdess, well, he would eat his cape. Fur and all.

Gwen's fluid movements caught him off guard. He tried to clear his throat, but found it was too dry, due in part to the fact that his mouth was gaping open.

Well, at least he was breathing.

Though he did have an inkling that his heart had in fact stopped around ten seconds ago.

"Gwen," he croaked.

Her hair was piled high above her head, giving him a delightful view of her neck and high cheekbones. Her costume, while all white, had him forgetting his name.

The dress was by all standards proper, except for the fact that her sleeves fell effortlessly below her shoulders. Exposing so much skin his eyes hurt.

To stare at her was certain blindness. For everywhere he looked, he saw pure white skin, skin that had never been touched by any man, skin that invited him in by its very essence.

He reached out to touch her creamy white shoulder, but was immediately hit with a cane.

"Ah, the shepherd's crook. I forgot." He rubbed his shoulder where Gwen had tapped him.

They both wore masks, but hers did nothing to hide the beauty of her eyes, crystal blue eyes looking directly through him. Perhaps he should avoid staring at them lest he become entranced in their spell.

She hooked her arm into his. "Now, where shall we do this?"

Hunter tripped and cursed. "Sorry, the cape has a mind of its own." He looked away and rolled his eyes, quite certain that he had, in fact, just blamed his inability to walk in a straight line on an inanimate object.

Hunter touched his own mask to make sure it was still secure. "Now, what exactly did you have a mind to do?" He pulled at his cravat as it choked him even more, and waited.

"Our little talk, of course. I wish to know what you know. No more secrets."

"Dance with me," he said, quickly pulling her into his arms.

Soon they were matched up for a quadrille. "Really, your grace, must you be so dense?"

The man to Hunter's left coughed.

When he and Gwen touched hands again he whispered, "Have a care, we are in public."

"Thank you for reminding me."

Hunter nodded emphatically, and took a step back only to join her once more.

"Had you not reminded me," Gwen continued, "I would have accosted you where you stand for being such an idiot."

"Tell me," Hunter murmured as they turned. "Would that have been before or after you kissed me?"

Gwen gasped and stepped back.

Amused, Hunter winked and continued the dance.

When their hands met again, however, Gwen made a point to step on his toes harder than one ought, earning an earsplitting curse from him.

Ladies gasped.

Gentlemen chuckled, but the dance continued.

The minute it ended, Hunter grabbed Gwen's elbow and led her down the hall and up the back stairway.

Without speaking, he went to the first door and ushered her in, nearly pushing her to the ground in the process. "Is this a game to you?"

"Of course not!" Gwen leaned against her crook. Fire blazed behind those icy blue eyes. "I am your partner! If you keep things from me, how am I supposed to help?"

"I should ask you the same thing." Hunter said, his voice cool and detached.

"You. Are. Impossible. I do not even see why you are so special. What makes you the great Wolf of Haverstone? You haven't done a thing! While I've been thrust upon society like a tart!"

"Sweetheart, please do not compare yourself to such delicacies. At least tarts do not have fangs."

"Wolves have fangs."

"Believe me, I know." Hunter tilted his head to the side. "What is it you desire?"

"I want you to be real."

"And yet I stand before you, flesh and blood. I admit, you have me confused." Even as he said the words, he felt himself pale, felt the blood drain from his face. She asked too much of him. Women always did.

"For once." Gwen swallowed and walked toward him cautiously. "Leave the Wolf behind, take off the mask. Allow me to see you."

He cursed. "Why?"

"Because you are asking me to blindly trust a lie."

"And if the lie is better than the truth? What will you do?"

"Then I will have no choice but to trust the man."

"And the beast within?"

Gwen sighed. "Him as well."

It was one of those moments Hunter wished he could run away from. He could count on his one hand how many he had had in his lifetime. And they all had to do with his job as a spy and his role as a failed husband. They were moments that when one was held at gunpoint, one's treacherous mind replayed. Telling you, if only, and what you should have said, what you should have done.

With shaking hands, Hunter slowly reached up and pulled the mask away from his face.

"They are a joke, you know." He tucked the mask into his pocket and faced her head on. Allowing her to see the man few ever saw anymore.

"What are?"

"The idea of masks."

Gwen reached up and touched his face. He closed his eyes and pressed his lips to the inside of her wrist. She gasped. "Why is that?"

"I tell myself it hides reality, when in fact, I lost touch with reality long ago. The mask and I are one and the same, never to return to the shell of a man I was before. I am the Wolf, the Wolf is I, and Hunter… he died ten years ago."

"Why?"

"That, my dear, is the question. Why? Why live when death of one's heart and soul is so much less painful? For if I return to that place, I die all over again, and I'm too selfish to experience death twice."

"Now you speak in riddles." Gwen brushed the hair away from his forehead and kissed his chin.

"I speak in truths. The man everyone knows as the Duke of Haverstone ceased existing as a person the day he watched his other half, his soul mate, die in his arms."

For a moment, Hunter couldn't believe he had actually said all of that aloud, but he had no time to think. Voices interrupted his thoughts, so without pause he pulled Gwen behind the drapes and closed them. They were trapped between the balcony and the room, nothing but a bit of material hiding them and their costumes.

CHAPTER NINETEEN

Wolf—

I would not hold my breath if I were you. And if I've given you false hope, I sincerely apologize. My intention was to give you hades. Of course they both start with h so you can see my confusion. Apologies.

—Red

GWEN TRIED TO CALM her breathing as she heard the door open. The hushed voices grew louder as the footsteps approached the curtains and stopped directly in front.

"I always hated this house." The man sighed and touched the curtains directly in front of Gwen's face. Her breath hitched as Hunter jerked her closer to his body. She could feel every hard-planed muscle tense against her.

"Ah, Redding, do stop complaining. You are not the first man to despise these masquerades or this house. The decorations are less than to be desired. This much is true, old friend."

Redding? Old friend?

"Hollins, we are not, nor have we ever been, friends."

"Partners?" Hollins laughed. "Let us be partners then, for I believe I have some information you may find... interesting."

"Interesting how?" Redding sounded bored.

"Do you remember when you asked me a few months ago if anything was amiss at the War Office?"

"Of course." Redding scoffed. "It was not long after that that we became partners, as you call it."

"Precisely." Hollins cleared his throat. "I've made a new code. One that we will begin using immediately, starting this week, but I need you to become familiar with it before it is sent out. That way if I die, you will be able to continue in my place."

Silence, and then the feet shifted in front of Gwen and walked away. She exhaled and waited.

"Morbid but necessary," Redding said. "Well, what is it we are trying to communicate to the soldiers?"

"That, I cannot tell you just yet."

"Then what can you tell me?"

A few minutes went by and then Redding said, "I understand. I will meet you then."

Footsteps echoed across the floors and then the door clicked shut. Gwen peered around the curtain and saw that the room was empty.

"That was close," Hunter said from behind her, and then with a thud she fell to the floor as he pushed her out of the way.

Gwen opened her mouth to yell, but Hunter was on his hands and knees in front of the fireplace, where a piece of paper burned brightly.

"Help me," he ordered, as he pulled the paper from the fire and stomped on it. Gwen knelt down to look at it.

"I am sorry." She shook her head. "I cannot decipher it."

Hunter turned pale and cursed. "That is because it is in

code."

That following afternoon loomed. Gwen dreaded her meeting with Redding. Especially considering he was more than likely the man they were looking for. All signs pointed to him and Hollins; then again, Trehmont was just as slippery. But he hadn't made an appearance since Hunter called him out.

Truly it all gave her a headache. One could not simply call Bow Street upon suspicion of a crime. They needed evidence, and she had no idea how to gain any, short of waiting for one of the men to of course take a false step.

She pricked her finger on her needlepoint and sighed. Redding would arrive any moment, for he had specifically said that he would walk with her during the fashionable hour.

Oh joy.

The Montmouth butler, James, entered her sitting room and cleared his throat. "The Duke of Haverstone to see you, my lady."

What the devil was he doing here? He was going to ruin everything! Surging to her feet, she threw down her needlepoint and crossed her arms.

Hunter entered the room and gave her a weak smile.

Weak smile? Nothing was weak about Hunter's smile. Was he ill? What the blazes was wrong with him? Perhaps his gunshot wound was acting up?

"Hunter?" She narrowed her eyes. "Did you—" Truly she was losing her mind. "Did you cut your hair?"

"But of course. So glad you noticed." He winked.

She was convinced now, more than ever, that she needed to quit spying lest she finally lose her mind. "Hunter, I swear by all that is holy that if you do not be quick about what you came to say, I will strangle you with my bare hands! Redding will be here any minute, and we both know how important this meeting is!"

"Then I am right on time." Hunter approached her and took her hand in his. He smelled... different. Not unpleasantly so, but oddly like a stranger. She leaned in and sniffed again. No alcohol fumes? Is that why he looked so healthy?

"When you are done sniffing me, I will proceed." Hunter grinned.

Gwen leaned forward. "Your teeth, they look..." They were perfectly straight like Hunter's except the way his mouth formed around them was all wrong. His smile seemed wider and almost forced.

Hunter groaned. "Like teeth. Now, do stop getting distracted. This is important."

"Right." But Gwen could not for the life of her take her eyes away from Hunter's. That feature she knew about him. His eyes had always been an eerie golden brown, but right now they looked positively green! Impossible! She shook her head.

Hunter looked down, breaking his gaze. "You cannot go with Redding. Tell him you are unwell, tell him you find him lacking in some way, but do not get in the carriage with him. Do you understand?"

"No."

"Are you always this easy to get along with?"

Gwen laughed. "You of all people should know the answer to that question."

"I should. Shouldn't I?" Hunter leaned forward and caressed her face. "I see it. I did not think I would, but I see it. I see what the Wolf sees in you. Never lose your fight, love."

"Are you drunk?" Gwen leaned in. Perhaps there was whiskey on his breath?

"I wish I were; perhaps then this nightmare would finally

free me from its clutches." Hunter dropped her hand. "If you do not heed my advice, I will tie you up."

"Wouldn't be the first time," Gwen mumbled.

Hunter threw his head back and laughed. "I mean it, my lady."

"So now you call me a lady, after all we've been through? Not Red? Sheep? Nut or plain old Gwen?"

"Nothing about you is plain, my lady." He smiled warmly. "So I ask again, what will it be?"

"I will not stay."

"Then you leave me no choice." With a wicked smile he yelled at the top of his lungs. "My lady! Do you mind! I am not a piece of meat that you can throw yourself upon when you suddenly have an urge!"

"What are you doing?" Gwen hissed and smacked him on the arm. Insanity, it seemed, had finally caught up with her partner. Pity, she had always bet he would die of alcohol consumption first.

"My lady! Hands off!" Hunter smiled brightly. "I will not seduce you!"

"Hunter, I swear I will—"

"What the devil is going on?" Montmouth burst into the room.

"Ah, Montmouth is it?"

Idiot. He knew who Montmouth was.

"Kindly tell me why—" Montmouth looked from Gwen to Hunter. "Why, er, why she was thrusting herself upon you?"

"Other than the obvious?" Hunter clapped his hands together. "After all, what woman wouldn't be curious about my… talents?"

Montmouth lunged for Hunter, but Hunter quickly moved away.

"It would be wise, Haverstone, to be quick with your

explanation."

Hunter slowly walked to the door and stopped in front of Montmouth. "It seems your innocent little flower is not so innocent, for not but three minutes ago she threatened to kiss me. Apparently, the little girl wanted a bit of... rake."

"Leave," Montmouth said through gritted teeth. "Now."

"My pleasure, but do be careful about keeping her on a short leash. After all, Redding is on his way to take her on a walk. Wouldn't want her asking him the same favor. You could very well find her ruined."

Gwen watched in astonishment as Hunter ruined every single plan she had for that afternoon and possibly her life.

Upon Hunters exit, Montmouth slammed the door behind him and glared at Gwen. "What must I do to keep you safe from ruin? It seems you are even a danger to yourself!"

Gwen opened her mouth to speak, but Montmouth held up his hand. A large vein in his head began to throb as if it too was angry. So she kept quiet.

"You will not interrupt me, and you will not leave this house."

"For how long am I to be kept prisoner?"

"Until I die!" Montmouth yelled.

Gwen bit her lip to keep from shouting back.

Montmouth cursed. "I did not mean that." He cursed again. "Women are a plague."

"I'll be sure to tell my sister you think so."

"Brat." Montmouth smirked. "Please, I do not care for gray hair. At least stay in the house until your sister returns, and she can deal with you."

"You are passing me off?"

Montmouth strolled back toward the door. "With pleasure. I'll be sure to have the staff watch you."

Just then the butler approached the door. "Viscount Redding to see you, my lady."

"I will take care of this." And with that Montmouth left the room.

Gwen had trouble deciding if she was more upset or impressed with Hunter's acting ability. He better have a good reason for keeping her away from Redding and it better be a matter of life or death. If not, then she was going to shoot him.

CHAPTER TWENTY

Red—

Sometimes I imagine what your face would look like while reading these little love notes from yours truly. Do you blush? Does your body warm at the thought of my hands touching you? I find myself positively aroused thinking upon such things, which is why I think upon them often. Care to take a guess at what I'm thinking about doing to you now?

—Wolf

HUNTER POUNDED ON THE door for the third time. Earlier that morning he had sent a perfect copy of the code to his grandfather for him to decipher. He knew it was of the utmost importance that he give the man time to look it over. Considering their last meeting, he had reasons to believe Lainhart's mind was indeed weak. Hunter had given him three hours to look at the code. It should be long enough.

He knocked again.

Where was that blasted butler?

It was nearing the time when Gwen and Redding would

have their romantic walk, and he was planning on spying the entire time. He knew Gwen could take care of herself, but something about Redding did not sit well with him. Perhaps it was the idea that the man would be breathing the same air as Gwen. Not that he was jealous.

He pulled out his pocket watch and cursed. After one final knock went again unnoticed, he tried the door and pushed his way inside.

A maid was slowly walking down the stairway. "Apologies, it seems our butler has gone missing!"

"Clearly," Hunter said dryly. "I need to see Lainhart. We have a meeting of sorts."

"Of course. Just this way." She turned to go back up the stairs, but he caught her arm.

"Actually, I know where he is. I am, after all, his grandson."

The maid paled. "I'm so sorry your grace, I had no idea! I—"

"It is of no consequence. I will see myself the rest of the way to his room."

Nodding, she nearly ran back down the stairs as he quickly walked in the direction of Lainhart's room.

Without knocking, he burst into the room, his eyes scanning for the maid who usually attended to his grandfather. She was sitting by his side, and she was writing.

Lainhart looked up and pointed down. Not good.

"Has he had enough time to decipher it?" Hunter outwardly remained calm, even though his heart was pounding in his ears.

Lainhart pointed up while the maid nodded. "Yes, it seems part of the code was destroyed, but there is enough to see the location and time. There is also a smaller code near the corner of the paper that says something disturbing."

"And?"

Lainhart shook his head slowly and pointed down as he opened his mouth. "A-again."

The maid sighed. "He's been saying that all day. Again, again. I have no clue what he means, and he often falls asleep after he tries to speak. The exertion is hard on his frail body. I do not know how this will help but I wrote down what he was able to decipher."

She held out a note.

Hunter greedily took it. "My thanks. I have an appointment. I must be going."

"S-stop!" Lainhart wailed.

Hunter watched as his grandfather's mouth shook, his lips trying to form words that his body was no longer able to pronounce. "D-danger."

Sweat ran down Lainhart's cheek as he repeated the same word again and closed his eyes.

"I know, grandfather. I know." His eyes flickered to Lainhairt's hand. It twitched and then he pointed up and crossed his heart.

"What does that mean?" Hunter asked the maid.

She swiped a tear from underneath her eye and sighed. "A broken heart."

Anger and guilt slammed Hunter in the chest. Unable to breathe, he nodded and ran out of the room as fast as he could. He ran until he reached the front door and ran until he was in front of his carriage. All the while pushing the memory of what he'd just seen to the farthest point in his mind.

His fault.

He had broken the old man's heart.

And Lainhart had nothing to show for it. Nothing but a grandson by marriage who did exactly what Eastbrook had accused him of.

Abandoned his family, abandoned what was left of it, took up with the first whore he saw, and never returned to

London.

Until now.

He truly was a poison. Would he ever get life right? Or would he for the rest of his existence be in purgatory, hoping that when he did die, what he did on earth was enough to atone for the sin of being late? Of not being the husband he should have been?

He shoved his hands into his pockets, then suddenly remembered he had the note still clenched tightly within his palm.

Hunter unfolded the paper and read the location.

Hyde Park. Three in the afternoon. Bring Lady Gwendolyn, and then near the side of the note, just as the maid had said, was the word *death*.

"No, no..." His hands shook as he jumped into the carriage. "Hyde Park! As fast as you can!"

The carriage jolted to life, but all Hunter could think as he waited an eternity to arrive, was that he could not go on living if he was to be late a second time.

He would rather die.

Within minutes, he was at Hyde Park. He jumped, or rather flailed, out of the carriage and began running — not sure which direction to run into and not caring that he looked a complete lunatic. The note hadn't said which area of the park, and considering it was quite large, he would have a devil of a time locating them.

His eyes greedily scanned the park. Most people were too caught up in their own lives to notice that he was having a near apoplexy as he tried to locate Redding or the crest on his carriage.

Just when he was about to give up hope, he saw him.

Across the park, near the Corner, and laughing as he got into his carriage.

Hunter ran across the grass, his legs burning as his

muscles flexed and stretched.

An eerie sense of foreboding caused him to stop in his tracks as he watched the carriage drive away, and then explode. Pieces of debris went flying into the air as the horses neighed and galloped from the scene, both of them covered in dust. Blood was everywhere.

Hunter froze. Everyone around him screamed, women began running in every direction, men cursed and quickly herded people away from the disaster.

But Hunter was immobile.

Late. Again. His heart clenched. Funny, for he hadn't realized his still worked after breaking in two, but there it was, slamming into his chest and causing him more pain than he thought possible.

Hadn't he already lived through enough guilt?

Gwen was dead. And it was his fault. Because for the second time in his life, he was late and unable to stop catastrophe.

He choked back a sob and walked solemnly toward Montmouth's residence.

It was the same walk he had taken not nine years previous, when he'd had to announce to Lainhart that his granddaughter, his favorite little girl, had died.

Hollow. That's how he felt. As if his insides no longer existed. The only reason he knew he was still living was because he was in his own living Hell. And if he were dead, he would be reunited with Gwen, with Lucy. Instead, he was on his way to announce the death of one of the most brilliant women he'd ever known.

The carriage ride was too short.

The air too calm and peaceful.

Laughter echoed from inside, and Hunter argued with God for a minute. Why hadn't He taken him in her place? Why snuff out the life of someone so young, so beautiful? Why allow him to live through such horror twice? Perhaps this was his punishment; maybe he truly was in Hell and his reality was to live through the pain of loss for the rest of his existence.

Legs like lead, he walked slowly to the door and prayed Montmouth would just shoot him and put him out of his misery. It took more than five minutes for Hunter to keep his hands from shaking, and another two minutes to wipe the tears that had suddenly filled his eyes and spilled over.

He knocked softly on the door. Laughter from inside again mocked him, mocked what he was doing at this residence.

The door swung open.

With twinkling eyes, the butler nodded to him.

"Haverstone to see Montmouth. I have... news. It is urgent." He nearly choked on the last word. He had to control his emotions before they got the best of him. His lower lip trembled. He bit down to keep it from moving.

"But of course!" The butler nodded. "Though weren't you just here not but an hour ago?"

"No." Hunter walked into the house and sighed. "No, I was not."

"Are you sure?" The butler questioned him.

Irritated, Hunter snapped, "I'm sure! Now I need to see Montmouth!"

"Quite demanding for someone who just imprisoned me in my own home," came that sweet voice.

Hunter's head snapped up.

Gwen stood there, arms crossed and eyes blazing, as if she wanted to murder him where he stood. Which truly wasn't all that new.

"G-Gwen?" he sputtered. "Is it truly you?"

She rolled her eyes. "Must you always get yourself foxed before we have conversations?"

"Gwen?" he repeated again, this time walking toward her

with his arms open. A tear escaped his cheek before he could stop it. Exhaustion or perhaps madness set in, and he collapsed to the floor.

"Hunter!" Gwen raced to his side. "Rosalind!"

Hunter's blurry eyes took in Rosalind's form as she ran to his side and knelt to the ground, and then Montmouth rounded the corner and laughed.

He laughed.

"Did she clock you, then?" he asked.

Gwen scoffed. "I did nothing of the sort! He simply collapsed into a puddle at my feet!"

"Is he foxed?" Montmouth asked, as if Hunter wasn't having a real-life hallucination.

"He said not," Gwen answered, and then touched Hunter's forehead.

He reeled back and with a curse scrambled to his feet. "This is not real. I'm dreaming. I have to be dreaming."

Gwen laughed. "I believe we've been over this before, Hunter. I would never visit you in your dreams."

"But, but, the carriage... and Redding? Why are you not with Redding?"

The room fell silent.

Montmouth cleared his throat. "Did you hit your head during the fall?"

"No." Hunter couldn't take his eyes off Gwen. Was this real? Was she real? Or had he suffered through so much pain and agony that his mind was making up nonsensical things?

"Strange." Montmouth scratched his head. "Your hair. It is... well, it is quite long."

"What?" Hunter snapped out of his fog and glared at Montmouth. "What the devil does that have to do with anything?" He pointed at Gwen. "Why is she alive?"

Montmouth laughed. "Really, Haverstone, I'm not so much of an ogre that I would shoot my own sister-in-law for trying to seduce you."

Dreaming. He truly was dreaming. Gwen would rather seduce a cactus than him. He laughed bitterly at the joke and shook his head. "Right, and I'm Saint Peter."

Gwen poked him in the chest. "No, you're the devil himself! How dare you tell my brother-in-law that I tried to seduce you! And then keep me imprisoned in my own house! And then…" Gwen reeled back. "Why are you wearing different clothes, and why the devil is your hair longer?"

"That's what I said," Montmouth grumbled, and scratched his head. "Will someone please tell me what the blazes is going on?"

Gwen examined Hunter.

Hunter, possibly a little too excited to see her alive and breathing, did the first thing he could think of. He pulled her into his arms and kissed her.

In front of Montmouth, God, and everyone.

CHAPTER TWENTY-ONE

Wolf—

So you desire to know what I'm doing when I read these notes? I should think that the burning hole in the middle of this correspondence should suffice. To be quite honest, I read the note, offer my reply, then pull out my pistol and shoot it. But for some reason, the agitation and irritation do not leave me. You're like a plague; therefore, I burn every note. And while I watch the flames, do you know what I do? I smile.

—Red

HUNTER'S LIPS WERE FIRM against hers. Heat enveloped her body as he tugged her forcefully against him. Hands dipped into her hair causing a nervous fluttering in her belly.

His tongue slipped into her mouth.

His kiss, unlike previous kisses, was so tender, she fought the urge to gasp from the shock of it all.

With her heart beating erratically, she wrapped herself around his body, allowing her breasts to press against his firm chest.

"What the devil!" Montmouth shouted, pulling them apart, but Hunter just reached for her over Montmouth's hands, as if losing her touch was such a painful idea that he could no more release her than stop breathing.

"Do you mind!" Montmouth shouted again, this time punching Hunter in the stomach. Hunter doubled over, but as he fell, his hand reached out yet again toward Gwen.

She took it and held on. Much to the shock of the entire family, who stood with mouths gaping open, as if she had taken complete leave of her senses.

"Cease from touching one another!" Montmouth grumbled. "Now tell me what the blazes is going on before I lose my mind!"

"I cannot." Hunter straightened to his full height. "Up until a few minutes ago, I thought I was dreaming."

"Yes, well, up until a few minutes ago, I was considering allowing you to live." Montmouth narrowed his eyes and crossed his arms. "Now, explain why you would accuse Gwen of seducing you, leave, then return and pretend to have not been here. Everyone saw you. Saints alive! I spoke to you! Now, unless you have an identical twin waltzing around, you'd better explain. Now."

Gwen watched the color drain completely from Hunter's face. "Impossible." He paced in front of her, running his hands through his hair. "It cannot be. He is dead, or presumed dead! He disappeared the day she died, the day..." Hunter began to shake. "I think I need a drink."

"Would that make you feel better, then?" Montmouth asked.

"Immensely."

"Rosalind, hide the whiskey. Oh, and do send a note to Dominique. It seems we are to have a duel."

"A duel?" Gwen gasped. "Whatever for?"

"He kissed you." Montmouth shrugged.

"So you plan to shoot him?"

"My dear, I see no other option."

"Than death?"

Montmouth shrugged. The man shrugged! As if killing Hunter was the same as stepping on an ant!

"You cannot simply shoot him because he kissed me! Besides it wasn't even the first time!"

Rosalind gasped. Montmouth's face turned an interesting shade of purple, and though Hunter still appeared pale, a smug grin appeared on his face. Rogue.

"I'll kill him where he stands," Montmouth announced, eyes narrowing as he purposefully stepped toward Hunter.

Hunter, deciding against bravery, scooted over and stood behind Gwen. "I believe if you hear all of the facts, then you will be less likely to shoot me. Besides, I've already been shot once this week."

Gwen nodded. "True, he has been shot, but that was after I broke his nose."

"Not helping," Hunter murmured behind her.

"Five minutes." Montmouth held up his hand. "You have five minutes to explain before I lose my mind and shoot Hunter on irritation alone."

Gwen could feel the heat of Hunter as he stood behind her. His breath tickled her neck. She wanted nothing more than to lean against him and close her eyes. What was happening to her? She was supposed to be his partner. She refused to become attached to the type of man who would rather stare at himself in the mirror and smile than give any part of himself to a woman.

"I am not necessarily, er, retired." Hunter walked around Gwen and approached Montmouth, hands raised in surrender. "However, it would be best for us to continue this conversation in the privacy of your study."

Montmouth sighed and led the way. Hunter followed.

Rosalind linked her arm within Gwen's as they trailed behind the men.

Montmouth turned, starting to close the doors in front of the women's faces, but Gwen held her foot out, blocking it. "I think not. After all, I do not trust you alone with him. Who knows? You may slip and accidently shoot your pistol."

Curses exploded out of Montmouth's mouth. He looked to Rosalind as if to say, "Help!" but she merely tilted her head as if to say, "Give me a reason to slap you."

He held the door open wide for them to enter.

"You have ten minutes before I accidentally—" Monmouth glared at Gwen. "What did you say before? Oh, yes, before my finger accidentally slips on the trigger of my pistol."

Hunter looked at Gwen and winked. "I only need five."

Montmouth cursed. "I was discussing your story, not your speed at seduction."

"Apologies." Hunter nodded and gave Gwen another grin. Heavens, she felt heated all over. She fanned her face, much to Hunter's amusement.

He cleared his throat. "I came here to tell you Gwen had died."

"Clearly she lives," Montmouth spat.

"Are you planning on interrupting me the entire time?"

"Sorry."

Hunter took a seat. "An hour ago, I was not at your residence, but speaking with my grandfather. He has been helping me with a current assignment. As I said, I am not truly retired, at least not yet." Hunter sighed. "I went directly from our meeting to the park to save Gwen. I had reason to believe she was in danger. It seems Redding may have gotten himself into a bit of trouble, and she was to be with him on her walk. The minute I arrived, I tried to locate him, but was too late. For the minute his carriage began to drive away, it exploded."

Gwen gasped. "Is he alright?"

Hunter shook his head slowly from left to right. "I highly doubt there are any survivors. There was debris everywhere. Whoever placed the explosives did a deuced good job. I admit to being so..." his voice cracked, "upset, that I came here straightaway to deliver the news."

"Then explain the so-called twin who was here earlier. By the saints, he even acted exactly like you!" Montmouth shook his head in confusion and cursed again.

Gwen smiled to herself and whispered, "He did not smell the same."

"What was that?" Montmouth asked.

"Nothing." She looked to Hunter, and his eyes brightened. She wanted to touch him, to feel his lips on hers again. Was that why he'd kissed her? He'd thought she was some sort of ghost? Or were his true feelings finally showing through, since he'd thought he had lost her?

"I have a twin." Hunter cleared his throat and folded his arms across his chest. "But up until a few minutes ago, I thought him dead. I don't suppose he left a way to contact him?" Mask slipping, Hunter appeared eager to see his brother. It pained her heart to be of no help.

Gwen shook her head. "I am sorry, Hunter. I truly thought it was you. I did not think to ask, and I believe if I would have, he would have merely given me your information."

"Right." Hunter cursed. "Why would he appear here? Now? What did he say to you?"

Gwen felt herself turn red with both embarrassment and anger. "He accused me of trying to seduce him."

Hunter laughed.

Of course he laughed. The cad. "Apologies, Gwen. It is just that, well, you would not know how to seduce a man if he begged you."

"Care to give it a try?" she countered, stepping toward him, ready to rip his tight jacket straight from his body to prove a point. And to feel his lips on hers again, but first she would strangle him, of course.

"Easy." Montmouth placed a hand on her shoulder. "If you do not care to witness his death, you will cease from taking another step."

She took another step.

Hunter grinned wolfishly then beckoned her with his finger.

Montmouth turned his head just in time to see Hunter make the gesture and cursed. "It is like herding children! Must I separate you two?"

"If you must." Hunter relaxed into the chair. "But know that it only makes finding her that much more… rewarding."

Gwen scowled and began searching for a weapon. If she could not prove her point, she would simply force him to admit she was just as skilled as he. Besides, she knew how attached he was to that handsome face of his. All she needed was a knife, a dagger, a rusty nail…

"Am I to understand that my dead brother resurrected himself, somehow read the code that was safely in my grandfather's possession, pretended to be me, and then accused our dear innocent Gwen of taking advantage?"

"Yes, that sounds right," Gwen said through clenched teeth. "Though it pains me to admit there are two of you in this world."

"Clearly our masculinity offends you."

"Your entire being offends me, Wolf."

"Have a care what you say… Red."

"Pet names?" Montmouth sputtered. "You have pet names for one another?"

Hunter shrugged.

Gwen refused to take her eyes away from his. If he was

going to be difficult, then she was going to be the thorn in his side. He winked and licked his lips as if he were staring at a tasty morsel.

"...After all, it pains me to admit there is just nothing more that can be done," Montmouth said. Had he been talking? Blast. Why did Hunter have to have such plump lips? And beautiful eyes, truly beautiful. Not the type that looked feminine in any way, but dangerous — mystical even. His grin set his eyes off, adding a spark of mischief and wickedness.

"...I believe the end of the week will suffice. Do you agree, Gwen?"

What was Montmouth asking?

Hunter raised his eyebrow, no doubt waiting for her to ask her brother-in-law to repeat his statement. Not wanting to look stupid, she merely nodded. "I could not agree more."

"Really?" Montmouth and Rosalind said in unison.

She looked to Hunter for help. But it was as if he had suddenly discovered he had hands, for all the intensity with which he was staring at them.

"Yes," she answered.

Montmouth was silent for a while and then scratched his head. "Well, in that case, I should see to making the proper arrangements. Come along, Rosalind. They should probably have a moment alone to speak. Though I will place your maid at the door. You have at least earned a few minutes for being so amiable after everything, my dear."

He walked over and kissed her forehead before leading Rosalind out of the room and closing the door behind him.

Hunter burst out laughing. "Tell me, Red, do you have any idea what you've just agreed to?"

"Of course."

"Truly?" His voice was suddenly in her ear. She quickly turned around and glared.

"Yes!"

"So stubborn." His eyes raked her from head to toe. "I like that in my... women."

"Women." Gwen snorted. "Typical; you would pluralize that statement. We all know your interest lies with several, not just one."

"Oh, I don't know about that." His smile disappeared as his golden eyes flickered to her lips. "I imagine there is one specific woman I very much desire to taste again." His hand cupped her face as his thumb rubbed her lower lip and then his mouth was on hers.

Previous irritation with the man faded as his lips worked against hers. His hands caressed her neck and moved further down. She trembled against his touch as the warmth of his tongue singed her.

Too soon, Hunter pulled back. "What shall we tell Wilkins?"

"About Redding?" she whispered hoarsely, leaning shamelessly closer to him, craving the touch of his lips more than her next breath.

He kissed her softly, this time trailing his tongue along her lower lip before coaxing her head against his and wrapping his arms around her.

She moaned into his mouth.

He retreated and chuckled softly. "No, Red. About our marriage."

CHAPTER TWENTY-TWO

Red—

    So I irritate you? Is that it? At least I invoke some sort of strong emotion within you. Though I swear to you, by the end of the Season you will be begging for my kiss, longing for my touch, and if you are lucky, I may just give you exactly what your body burns for. And more. Now, you may shoot this letter out of anger; you may burn it out of pride. But tell me, what will you dream of when you close your eyes? That's what I thought. Sweet dreams, Little Red...
        —Wolf

HER KISS IGNITED SOMETHING long dead within him. It had always been that way with Gwen, absolutely explosive. As if they could not have a normal conversation without pulling out some sort of weapons, and when they were not fighting, they were flirting. Whether it be with their words or their actions. It was impossible to quit the woman.

Now he wasn't so sure he wanted to.

But marriage? It would be a cold day in Hades.

He'd tried that once. And failed miserably. Though he

hadn't the heart to embarrass her in front of her family. He would simply allow her to cry off. No doubt she would have a fit when she heard the news, but her lips were so blasted tempting, and he had thought her dead.

So he'd kissed her.

And now, the look on her face, one of pure horror and not elation, made his decision all the more simple. After all, marriage was impossible for a man who'd lost the other half of his soul long ago.

"Marriage?" she repeated, taking a step back.

"But of course!" He laughed. "You agreed to it. I was here. I would know. By the by, you were also present. Wonder what you found so blasted distracting?" He brought his hand to her face and then trailed it down her neck, stopping just above her breasts.

She slapped it away. "I must think, and I cannot do that when you are..."

"Seducing you? Kissing you? Touching, begging, biting, tasting..."

"Breathing!" she yelled and pushed against him, but he held her firmly in his embrace.

"Never worry, my dear, all you need to do is cry off. It will not be so hard. Standing up to that giant of a duke will be good for you. Yes?"

"But..." Gwen chewed her lower lip. Blast, how he hated it when she did that. It made him want to kiss her more, and if he kissed her more he might just change his mind about marriage.

Sharing her bed every night was a temptation of gigantic proportions, and he was still a man. A broken one, at that.

"No." Gwen shook her head. "I cannot do it."

"My thoughts precisely. We cannot marry." Hunter should feel glad that she agreed with him, but instead felt nothing but emptiness. It was as if she had died all over again.

He released her and stumbled back, fighting with every ounce of strength he had left to look happy when inside he was slowly crumbling into dust.

He tried to smile again, but he felt it did not reach his eyes. He laughed mockingly at himself, cursed, and turned around. Where the devil was his mask when he needed it most?

"You misunderstand me, Hunter." Gwen took a step toward him and lightly touched his arm. "We must marry."

He looked down at her delicate fingers as if they burned a hole of desire straight through his jacket. "We cannot."

"It is the right thing to do. Be reasonable! You have kissed me quite soundly in front of our entire staff. Not to mention my sister and brother."

"A secret." His voice shook. "We could keep it a secret. Pay off the staff..."

"And lose your honor in the process?" Gwen tilted her head. "Besides, weren't you the one who said we had crossed so many lines already?" The minx brought her hand up to her dress and pulled the sleeve down.

What the devil was she doing?

She smirked. "We are attracted to one another, that much is true."

His eyes never left the exposed skin of her shoulder as it radiated promises of velvet smoothness and desire.

"And..." She reached to her other sleeve and tugged it down. "It will allow us to work more closely together. After all, your brother has risen from the dead, yet is still missing. You are being shot at, and for all we know, Redding is dead as well."

The woman had a point. Besides, if he married her, she would be under his watch, which also meant she would be under his care. She would want things. Things like children, and a happy home — his soul.

Yet he had nothing to offer her but his protection.

Perhaps that would be enough. It would have to be.

Gwen reached for him and placed her hands on his chest. "It is a brilliant idea."

He closed his eyes and moaned. "It is an attraction. Are you willing to base a marriage on that alone?" Even as he said it, he knew it was much more, but he wasn't willing to speak it aloud, lest his worst fears became realized. That he had fallen again, and this time, there was nothing to catch him but the cold, hard ground. Because in the end, he would not be enough. He would fail, and he hated to think of what would happen when he did.

"Yes," she answered, boldly kissing him across the mouth. "I am." Her tongue, all velvet sweetness, plunged into his mouth and tangled with his.

If he hadn't been convinced earlier, he was now. For his hands had a mind of their own as they tugged harder on her sleeves. Why wasn't she naked already? Why hadn't they sealed their agreement, and where had she learned to…

"Oh, my—" Her legs wrapped around his body as he lifted her against him and deepened the kiss.

"Gwen, I—"

The door flew open.

Montmouth yelled something, most likely a curse or a threat, but Hunter was too focused on Gwen's mouth.

"Release her or I will shoot you before your wedding day. I believe I have been gracious enough, giving you five minutes."

Hunter set Gwen down and grinned. "Told you it only took five."

Montmouth sputtered. "You seduced her, then?"

"No." Hunter took a step back, needing the distance air would give him. "She seduced me."

Gwen grinned proudly. "It took me two."

"Two?" Montmouth repeated. "Two what?"

"Minutes." Hunter walked by him. "I will see you tomorrow. We have arrangements to make for our... wedding."

CHAPTER TWENTY-THREE

Wolf—
Let us be honest with one another for once, shall we? I do not dream. If I allowed myself to dream, I fear I would not think on happy things but on war, blood, killing, and sacrifice. If you desire for me to be honest with you, then you must be ready to hear my confession. If you ever see me dreaming, please, have a care and wake me, for nightmares plague me in my sleep, and it seems the only thing able to scare them away is a living nightmare, in the shape of a wolf.

—Red

GWEN HAD TAKEN COMPLETE leave of her senses! What the devil had she been thinking? She hadn't. Not one logical thought had crossed her brain while she was in Hunter's arms.

That was the problem. She either wanted to strangle the man or kiss him senseless. Brilliant way to start a marriage. How long, she wondered, would they last before pistols were drawn?

Yet, she swallowed the lump of emotion in her throat, she

refused to shame her family further. Lies, so many lies, and all of them because of her, because she chose to keep a part of her life separate from her family. Because she chose to work in order to put food on the table after her father's murder the year previous.

She straightened her skirts and walked up to her room, closing the door behind her and leaning against it.

But Hunter? He had secrets as well, ones he thought he kept well hidden until his mask crumbled, leaving nothing in its place but the shell of a man broken. She wondered what would happen when he could no longer hide anymore. Would he ever love her? Come to care for her? Or would she always be cursed with this aching, this longing in the pit of her stomach for something more?

In a way, it made sense. Her sisters were both gifted with wonderful marriages. Rewarded for the lives they'd lived. While Gwen, well, she was going to marry a man who was more wolf than man. A gentleman who was more likely to have a wife and a mistress on the side, than to be loyal to one woman alone.

She touched her lips. Hunter's taste was still present. Gwen closed her eyes again.

A knock sounded at the door.

She stepped back and opened it.

"Oh good! No tears." Rosalind stepped into the room and shut the door firmly behind her. "Tell me you cannot seriously be willing to go into a marriage with a man who is better looking than any man has a right to be? Tell me you would like to cry off. All you need to do is say yes."

Gwen squinted. Hadn't her sister been in agreement with her husband?

"I see. No words. You must be in shock. Nod your head if you want to cry off."

Gwen bit her lip.

"Blink, can you at least blink? Oh heavens, where are the smelling salts! Is it possible to faint with one's eyes open?"

Gwen blinked several times and shook her head. "Have you lost your mind?"

"You ask me if I've lost *my* mind?"

Gwen nodded.

"Me?" Rosalind pointed at herself and laughed. "This from the woman who is days away from marrying the Duke of Haverstone? The Great Wolf? The same man who left a ball nearly naked nine years ago? They say he can speak over eleven different languages and has a mistress in every country! Even America!"

"Stop." Gwen couldn't hold the laughter back any longer. She wiped a tear of mirth away from her eye.

"See! You *are* crying!" Rosalind pointed an accusing finger her way.

"From laughter, yes." Gwen reached out and grasped her sister's hands within her own. "I know what I am doing. I truly do not want to bring shame upon my family. He has kissed me, several times if you must know. I set out to find a husband this Season and I landed a duke; why would I cry?"

"Because you do not love him." Leave it to Rosalind to pounce on the one thing that was bothering Gwen.

She released her sister's hands and straightened to her full height, which still did not match Rosalind's. "Sister, you are a romantic at heart. Your husband rode into your life on a white horse, literally."

Rosalind laughed.

"He pounded on the door and said he was going to rescue you and marry you. He danced with you in the meadow, he saved your life."

Rosalind began to pace, while Gwen continued her speech. "Isabelle was taken by the Beast, and his music spoke so richly to our sister that she was lost in him. She saved him, and in return his love for her is the strongest I've ever seen one human have for another." She took a shuddering breath. "What are the odds that that type of love would happen thrice in this family?"

Rosalind flushed and looked down. "It could happen. He looks at you…"

"Like any man would look at a woman he is attracted to." Gwen shrugged. "Sister, I know it is difficult for you. But you need to understand, there isn't always a white horse. There isn't always a faraway kingdom and a castle. Sometimes there is no one to save. And sometimes, the princess has to marry the mask before there will ever be hope to love the man."

"The mask?" Rosalind asked. "Whatever do you mean?"

"I imagine Hunter as a little boy lost in the woods. When he first set out on his trip, he had someone to fight for, something he was running toward, and when that thing shattered before his eyes, he became lost. He fell into himself and confused himself, for the monster had destroyed what he loved so dearly. He is both Hunter and Wolf. Beast and man, and he is lost. Therefore, even if he loved me or said he loved me, it would not be the type of love you experience. To ask for his love right now would destroy what shred of humanity he still possesses, and I love him…" Gwen closed her eyes and crossed her arms protectively around her chest. "I love him too much to ask for it."

Rosalind's face broke out into a bright smile. "You love him?"

"I am not sure. I mean, does love feel like you want to both kiss and strangle the object of your affection? Does it create so much unrest within your own body that you feel you are losing your mind? Is love so strong that I have a perpetual head and stomachache?"

"I had a headache for three days when I met Stefan." Rosalind smiled and looked down. "I also had several fantasies of hitting him across the head with his own pistol."

"I've had that one, as well." Gwen sighed happily. "I am not sure if my love trumps my desire to cause physical harm to his person. Most of the time he drives me so crazy I merely react out of frustration rather than love, but I imagine Hunter does not understand any other way to communicate than fighting and innuendo."

"He's a man." Rosalind shrugged as if that explained everything.

The room fell silent.

Rosalind pulled Gwen into a tight hug. "Sister, it will not be easy, loving a wolf. The minute you get close, they tend to snap. Just remember it is out of defense, for a wolf fears man. Men are always a symbol of death for animals. Therefore you must tread carefully." Rosalind released her and sighed.

"Have no fear, dear sister. Wolves also love the thrill of the chase, the smell of blood and meat. I imagine my trap will be sufficient for him. And if all else fails, I'll merely take off my dress and use his own lust against him."

"Brilliant!" Rosalind clapped her hands. "Now, we only have a few days. Let us get our trousseau together. We shall stop by Isabelle's. Would you like me to tell her the news, or would you like to announce to your sister and the Beast that you are marrying one of their dearest friends?"

"I nominate Hunter."

"Good girl." Rosalind winked.

CHAPTER TWENTY-FOUR

Red—

I too dream of blood. I dream of killing, of lies, of violence and greed. But most of all, I dream of her. Of how I could not reach her in time. Dreams are a cruel thing, for this certain dream gives me hope that one day I will be on time, one day I will save her from death. Yet it always ends the same. I am holding her body in the street, and she is gone.

—Wolf

AFTER LEAVING MONTMOUTH'S RESIDENCE, Hunter made his way toward Wilkins' establishment. If he wasn't already privy to the information surrounding Redding's accident, then he needed to be. The last person to see Redding alive was most likely Hollins.

It took a half hour to reach the townhome.

The wind whipped Hunter's jacket around him as he made his way toward the stairs. He knocked twice.

No answer.

He knocked again.

Still no answer.

Biting back a curse, Hunter walked back to his carriage and made his way toward Dominique's residence. Now would be probably a better time than most to announce to the man that he was, in fact, marrying his wife's sister.

Perhaps he should send ahead a note to make sure all weapons were hidden.

Hunter grinned just thinking upon it.

Truly he should be anything but amused at this point.

Someone had shot at him, his dead brother was very much alive, a murderer was on the loose, and Redding was dead.

Yet all his ridiculous brain could think upon was the taste of Gwen's lips, the way her soft body felt pressed against his.

He told himself to stop grinning. That it was ridiculous and quite rude, considering a man had died today.

But it could not be helped. He looked at the dreary streets of London and for once his mood did not match what he saw. No, the blasted world could be coming to an end, and he would still be in his carriage, smiling.

The carriage pulled to a stop in front of Dominique's townhouse. Hunter cleared his throat and tried to think upon what he needed to do. The minute he pressed his lips together another grin broke out.

It was useless.

Which was why, when Samuel the infuriating Russian butler opened the door, Hunter felt the need to finally get the man's name right rather than irritate him beyond reason.

"My good man." He slapped the butler on the back. "Is the Beast at home?"

Samuel groaned and rolled his eyes. Perhaps it was impossible for Hunter to be normal. Perhaps it was because the man was Russian, which immediately made Hunter want to say something annoying. After all, he was conditioned to do so with all Russians; just ask Dominique.

"In the study." Samuel pointed and wandered off.

"Thank you," Hunter yelled at the retreating butler's back. A grunt was his only response.

Hunter sauntered over to the study and knocked on the door.

No answer.

Was no one at home today?

And then he heard it.

A blunt object was suddenly pushed against the back of his head and the all-too-familiar click of the hammer being pulled back gave him pause.

"Explain," Dominique said in Russian.

He only spoke in Russian when he was truly upset.

"Has something happened?" Hunter asked in English.

"It is about to," Dominique ground out. "You have three seconds."

"Listen—"

"One."

Hunter tried to turn around, but Dominique pushed him against the wall.

"Two."

"Fine!" Hunter held up his hands and cursed. "What is it you want? And stop pointing that thing at my head! Devil take it, you are not even giving me a chance to speak!"

"One cannot speak if one is dead." Dominique cursed in Russian, then pulled the pistol back from Hunter's head. Though the minute the pressure was relieved, he kicked Hunter in the leg, causing a shooting pain to run from his calf all the way up his spine.

"What the devil is wrong with you?" Hunter flipped around and glared at his friend.

"I should ask you the same." The pistol was still pointed at Hunter's body. Brilliant. Perhaps he would get shot twice in one week! One could only hope.

Hunter could not fight back the grin. Truly, it was the worst time in the history of his lack of self-control to actually be unable to restrain himself.

"If you took advantage of her, slept with her, I swear I will shoot you and never look back." Dominique sneered. Ah, so he was to negotiate with a beast.

Well, he was a wolf, after all.

With a quick movement, he knocked the pistol out of Dominique's hand. It fell to the floor in a clatter as Hunter punched Dominique in the stomach. Was it his fault his fist slipped and nailed his best friend on the chin?

Cursing, Dominique came at him, fists flying. Within seconds they were on the floor wrestling one another.

"Heavens, what is all that noise?" came Isabelle's soft voice, and then the woman cursed. "Unhand each other this instant."

Dominique looked up at his wife. Hunter took advantage and landed a blow to his friend's jaw. Murderous outrage reflected in Dominique's face as he thrust his head against Hunter's, causing his body to slump to the cold hard marble.

"Isabelle? What is all that noise?" Another figure appeared. Though the voice was feminine, Hunter could not be sure if it was another person, or if he was suffering merely from double vision.

"Dominique!" Gwen yelled. "Kindly remove yourself from my future husband!"

"Not until he's dead." Dominique cursed and grasped at Hunter's cravat, winding it tightly into his hand. To breathe was the very devil. To be fair, Hunter hadn't expected this reaction from Dominique. Now, Montmouth? That was another story entirely.

"I said release him." Gwen pushed Dominique off of Hunter and glared. "Truly, what has gotten into the both of you? Acting like rebellious children! Whatever happened to talking?"

Hunter pointed at Dominique. "He tried to shoot me."

"He struck me first!" Dominique argued.

"And my horse is bigger than yours," Isabelle said dryly. "Now, husband, explain." She glared daggers at Dominique. Hunter shifted nervously on the floor, suddenly feeling quite lucky that he wasn't married.

"He ruined her." If Dominique pointed his finger one more time in Hunter's direction, he was going to snap it in half.

"Actually..." Gwen winked at Hunter. "It is I who ruined him... for all other women."

There it was. That blasted grin. Though his face hurt like the devil, it decided to make an appearance again as his eyes greedily took in Gwen and her defense of him.

"And it only took two minutes," Hunter added helpfully.

"At most." Gwen sighed.

"What the devil is going on? And Hunter, I swear by all that is holy, if you lie to me, I will end you." Well, at least the bloke was speaking in English now. That had to be a good sign, didn't it?

"I'm a spy!" Gwen blurted, just as Hunter opened his mouth to speak. Was she planning on saving him all day or was this just a phase?

"Your grace." Samuel cleared his throat, taking in both bloodied men sitting on the floor, and shrugged. "This came for you while you were out."

Hunter winced as he rose to his feet and took the letter. He carefully opened it and cursed.

Redding dead. Meet tonight at 7, The Horse and Hare.

"Dead," Hunter mumbled and looked directly at Gwen. She paled and nodded her head just once.

"We only have two left. Two men." He held back the

information about Hollins and Wilkins. She did not need to know the specifics. If anything, he wanted to keep her in the dark. He wanted her alive. "It is imperative that we find out who it is, Gwen, especially considering we are to be married."

Ignoring the gaping mouths around him, Hunter walked over to Gwen and kissed her hand. "We will find him. We have to."

"But you were shot and..." Gwen shuddered.

Hunter sighed and pulled her into his embrace.

She exhaled softly. "You were afraid of losing me. You thought you had. But what—" Her voice caught. "What if I lose you?"

"Wolves are like cats, love. They have nine lives."

"—though I imagine he's outlived all of his," Dominique interjected. "Now, will someone please explain why you two seem so familiar, and why Gwen felt the need to lie about being a spy in order to save you, Hunter?"

"She didn't lie." Hunter released Gwen and turned toward Dominique and Isabelle. "But perhaps this is not the time."

"It is never a good time for one's lies to unfold," Dominique said through clenched teeth.

Isabelle cleared her throat. "Gwen? Why don't we let Rosalind know we are ready for Bond Street? I imagine she's finished taking her tea."

Gwen looked at Hunter and gave him a nod of approval as she walked off with Isabelle, leaving Dominique glaring at Hunter like a madman.

"Oh, do stop glaring. You'll give yourself a headache."

"Too late." Dominique cursed. "Though I blame you, not the glaring." He pinched the bridge of his nose. "I imagine this will take whiskey and a whole lot of talking. White's?"

Hunter sighed in relief. "Best idea you've had all afternoon."

Hunter fidgeted with the glass in his hand as Dominique took another sip. "I imagine you want me to apologize for pointing a pistol at your head."

"That would be nice."

"Forget it." Dominique cursed. "How was I to know the entire story? Is her family aware of her activities for the Crown?"

Hunter set the glass down and leaned back into the plush leather of the chair. "If they did not before, they will soon."

"Hmm." Dominique lifted the glass to his lips and winced as he took a swig. "Does she know?"

"Know?" Hunter repeated.

"About Lucy."

All it took was the mention of his dead wife's name and the smile, the one that had become a permanent fixture on his face during the entirety of the afternoon, faded away. "Not everything."

"And Ash?"

"Somewhat. Only that I had a twin brother I thought dead, nothing more."

Dominique set his glass down and leaned forward. "I imagine I am the last person you would ever think to give marriage advice, but it would be wise for you to tell her of your past, sooner not later."

The smile had turned into a frown as Hunter thought of his past, of the gory details. Was he ready to be that vulnerable with another human being? Dominique knew all his secrets, but up until a few months ago, he'd had his own demons to face.

Now it seemed that Hunter was alone in his darkness. It would be life's cruelest joke to find another woman in his life only to bring her down into the pit he so casually resided in.

"And if I cannot tell her?" he finally asked, not wanting to look Dominique in the eyes as he said it.

A sigh escaped Dominique before he picked up his whiskey and took another long swallow. "Then you may as well leave again."

"Leave?"

"Yes, leave. As in quit the continent. My friend, you do not want to live in a marriage that is one-sided. Where the woman you care about gives of herself until it hurts, where you hold back pieces of who you are. In the end, it will end in the death of her spirit and the death of your soul. Your marriage deserves the best chance it can get. All things considered, by not telling her of your past, you shoot yourself in the foot before you take one step toward that altar."

"When did wisdom suddenly give you the benefit of its blessing?"

Dominique chuckled. "Easy, I married her."

"Cheers." Hunter held up his glass. "To women."

With a laugh and a clink, Dominique finished his glass. "To women!"

"Huzzah!" a few men shouted behind them.

Conversation shifted to Dominique and his family, as well as Hunter's upcoming nuptials, but as much as Hunter tried, he couldn't find the smile that had plagued him before. The pressure of the world seemed to cave onto him. The minute Dominique had opened his mouth and spouted off all that ridiculousness about being honest with one's wife was the minute Hunter found it not only difficult to breathe but also blasted hot.

It was not fair to keep such things from Gwen, but fear has its way of keeping him from moving forward.

In that moment, Hunter saw everything within his reach. A woman who would both challenge and ignite him. A life filled with the comfort of being around his friends. The life that, not nine years ago, he had lusted after and strived for was once again within his reach.

So why couldn't he have it? What was causing this panic?

Nine years ago, he had felt happy, free, his smile as wide as it had been today, and in an instant he had lost it all.

When God chose to bless a person, it was both frightening and wonderful. For one had to wonder, when everything was going right, when everything was perfect, were you only one step away from disaster?

Excusing himself early, Hunter left and went in search of the Horse and Hare. He knew what he had to do. He had to solve the mystery of the ciphers now. If not, he shuddered to think of what hung in the balance.

His future happiness and Gwen's depended on his success and this time, he would not fail.

CHAPTER TWENTY-FIVE

Wolf—

I imagine she is quite content to be in your dreams. Perhaps you should think upon that instead of the blood and death. Think of the very idea that this woman, this love, is in your dreams every night, exactly where she desires to be, for dreams are directly connected to one's heart. And it seems that her heart is yours for the taking.

—Red

THE ESTABLISHMENT WAS POORLY lit and filled with more drunks than Hunter cared to surround himself with.

He quickly moved through the crowds of gentlemen slapping one another on the back and belching, and sat down.

"You're early," a voice said behind him. Was everyone sneaking up on him these days? Perhaps retirement truly was in the cards for him.

He waited until Wilkins sat down across from him.

Wilkins looked quite normal for having just lost a very important part of his case. "Redding is dead, as you well know."

"Yes, which only leaves us Hollins, considering we traced a smuggling ring back to Trehmont; nothing there."

"I would not discount Trehmont." Wilkins appeared thoughtful. "After all, he is just desperate enough for the money to do it."

Hunter nodded. "But he has been making quite a lot of blunt from his smuggling. Why would he need more?"

Wilkins shrugged. "Greed. A person always wants more. Wouldn't you agree?"

Something shifted in the air. Hunter examined Wilkins' face. He appeared tired, but not upset or even depressed that he had lost Redding.

"I am sorry about Redding. If I would have been there sooner..." Hunter trailed off.

Wilkins waved him away. "It is not your fault. Besides, it is possible that he was the spy in the first place. In fact..." He reached into his jacket pocket and pulled out a few notes. "We found these at his residence."

"What are they?" Hunter picked up each sheet of paper. Codes littered the front of them. Obviously it was impossible to decipher them without his grandfather's help.

"Proof."

"Of?"

"Treason." Wilkins shook his head. "Though I hate to see Redding take the fall. He was, after all, a decorated hero and a good man. The money must have been too hard to pass up."

"Right." Hunter looked closely at the codes and noticed that the tiny symbols did not resemble the first note he'd received. "And you say these are perfect copies of the notes given to the front lines?"

"Absolutely." Wilkins grimaced and rose to his feet. "Keep them for now. If you would like to have them deciphered, that is fine by me. They are, after all, old news."

Hunter stuffed the codes into his pocket. "Is that all?"

"This investigation is over, for now." Wilkins rose to his feet. Hunter grabbed his arm, motioning for him to wait.

"It is about Red." He scratched his head. "It seems I have compromised her."

"Her cover is blown?" Wilkins whispered.

"I did not compromise her in that capacity." Hunter looked away, suddenly embarrassed. "I *compromised* her, if you get my meaning."

"Tossed her skirts, did you?"

Oh, how he wished! "Not yet, though I came close."

"Wouldn't be the first time someone was interested in that little delicacy, believe me. How do you think the woman was able to infiltrate into Napoleon's elite so quickly?"

Hunter saw red. He clenched his fist and pounded the table. "Never speak of her in that way again. She is to be my wife."

"Is she?" Wilkins smiled, and then chuckled, and finally threw his head back and gave in to full-on laughter. "This is more perfect than I could have imagined it."

"Perfect?" Hunter's fist was still clenched. He was seconds away from flattening the man.

Wilkins wiped his eyes and shook his head. "Yes, well. Congratulations are in order, good fellow. When is the wedding?"

"Special license, three days."

"Are you resigning?" Wilkins asked.

Was he? Why were things so complicated? "Yes, I believe I am."

"I remember when you resigned the first time, and look how that turned out."

Hunter jerked to his feet and glared. "Explain yourself."

Wilkins took a step back from Hunter. His eyes never wavered as he looked him up and down. "Just reminding you of what happens when you allow your emotions to rule your decisions, friend."

Cursing, Hunter ran his hands through his hair and looked away. "Are we done?"

"More than you know, Hunter. More than you know." With that, Wilkins walked off, leaving Hunter more confused than ever. Yet the weight on his chest was lifted. He was doing the right thing. His priorities were straight. For the first time in nine years, the guilt that had weighed so heavily on his heart did not seem so heavy. A fresh start. He had been given a fresh start.

He pulled out the codes again. Something wasn't right about the way the symbols were drawn. They reminded him of the last note Redding had had in his possession. There had been two codes on that note. Redding would have only understood one.

Hollins had led Redding to his death. Hunter was sure of that now. But what did Wilkins have to do with everything? What wasn't he telling Hunter? He could not be trusted, and now that he was closing the investigation, things seemed more suspicious. Redding could not have possibly been the mole, or could he? Perhaps Wilkins had suspected Redding and Hollins had carried everything out, and then when they had discovered he was bad, they eliminated him. So why go to so much trouble to hire Hunter and Gwen to discover the traitor?

His head hurt. To make matters worse, he was to be married in three days. He only hoped he would make it to the wedding without getting shot or worse, killed.

CHAPTER TWENTY-SIX

Red—

I think that is the kindest thing you have ever said to me. Care to repeat it? Perhaps you like me more than you did a few weeks ago? Admit it. You care. I'm waiting for the words you're dying to say. The phrase is something like this, "I am in love with a wolf."

—Wolf

GWEN STARED AT HER reflection in the mirror and practiced her smile. She had to appear happy instead of afraid. For heaven's sake, she was a spy! Acting should come naturally, but the minute the last button was fastened on her dress, she began to panic. Her hands shook and everything became fuzzy in front of her.

What was she doing? Willingly walking down the aisle toward the man who had the power to destroy her or save her with one breath? Her eyes gave her away, and Hunter would know it the minute he saw her. He would see her hesitation.

She blinked several times, and tried to think of the benefits of marrying someone who was more beautiful than any man she had ever come across before in her existence.

He kissed well. She laughed to herself. *Well* did not even begin to describe what that man could do with his mouth.

His eyes were hypnotizing.

His hands, well... she shivered and bit her lip.

His laugh, his easygoing manner, and finally the pain he tried to hide behind every second of every day.

Marriage to Hunter would be the scariest and possibly one of the stupidest decisions she had made yet. At the end of the day, there was no one else's arms she would rather be in.

"Ready?" Rosalind burst into the room, Isabelle following close behind.

They'd insisted on more than just a private ceremony, but still only invited around fifty close friends.

"As I'll ever be." Gwen turned to them and smiled, hoping that she looked convincing and not like she was about to burst into tears at any second.

"You look beautiful." Isabelle grasped her hands and sighed. "I am so glad you decided to wear a bit of red. It looks like you."

Gwen laughed. "It will shock him, that much is certain." She glanced at her reflection again. The dress was ivory, with silver embellishments around the capped sleeves trailing all the way down her back. The silver-encrusted design also twirled about her sleeves and ended right below her breasts, creating a beautiful design of flowers. It was beautiful, gorgeous actually, but it had needed something. So she'd put a red ribbon in her hair.

The ribbon would match her red cape as well as her red roses. Hunter would probably have a heart attack when he saw her, thinking she was getting married in red, but she felt more like herself, more comfortable this way.

In a way, it was a sign for him. She needed him to see that he was not only marrying the woman the ton saw as Lady

Gwendolyn, but also the spy Red. She was both people, just as he was both Hunter and Wolf.

"Beautiful." Rosalind sighed behind her. "Now, you've kept him waiting long enough. In an hour, you will be a married woman!"

Gwen swallowed the emotion in her throat and followed her sisters out the door and down the stairs.

The wedding was being held at a small chapel on the back of Dominique and Isabelle's estate in town. With a deep breath, she walked toward her future.

"What the devil is taking her so long?" Hunter paced in front of Montmouth and Dominique.

"If I didn't know any better, I'd say the great Wolf was a bit nervous." Dominique chuckled and elbowed Montmouth, who still looked like he was just waiting for the opportune moment to shoot Hunter in the face.

"Oh, do stop glaring," Hunter mumbled to Montmouth.

"I am not glaring, I am merely…" He cursed and joined Hunter in his pacing. "She is my responsibility. I just need to know I am doing the right thing."

"Too late to go back now." Dominique looked at Montmouth and then Hunter. "By the by, when did I turn into the optimistic one of the group?"

This received a much needed chuckle from both Montmouth and Hunter.

Rosalind poked her head into the room adjacent to the main chapel and announced, "It is time!"

Hunter suddenly felt ill.

"Not the best time to lose your nerve." Dominique grinned. "Now, go, it seems you have a bride waiting to marry you."

Montmouth and Dominique led the way out of the room. Hunter followed and then took his place at the head of the aisle, next to the vicar.

He should be excited, but memories of his first wedding overwhelmed his brain, making it impossible to focus on anything.

Lucy had worn blue.

Her eyes had shone with tears. Her grandfather had refused to walk her down the aisle on the principal that she was marrying a rogue.

Eastbrook had done the honors.

It had been the happiest day of his life.

How could he have known that their first anniversary would result in her death? That the light that danced in her eyes would be dead in another three hundred and sixty-five days?

His hands shook; he folded them behind him. The last thing Hunter wanted was for Gwen to think he was regretting the decision to marry her. If anything, it wasn't regret; no, it was more like fear. No, absolute terror. God had given him another woman, another responsibility, and he would rather die than for her to suffer the same fate as Lucy.

The doors opened.

Gwen emerged.

In a red cape.

He burst out laughing, causing quite a few loud whispers to rise within the small chapel.

With a wink, she took off the cape, revealing a beautiful ivory dress fit for a princess. He did not deserve the way she looked, nor the twinkle in her eyes when she pointed to the ribbon in her hair and grabbed the red roses from the basket Montmouth held out to her.

The music began, she took a step on Montmouth's arm, and then the doors opened again.

His eyes had to be deceiving him, for the man who came into the chapel was Lainhart.

And his butler was with him, looking as shaggy as ever. Did the man ever shave? Or bathe for that matter? The butler pushed Lainhart's wheeled chair in front of Montmouth and then spoke in hushed tones.

Montmouth jerked his head back and then asked Gwen a question. She nodded her head yes and kissed Montmouth on the cheek, and then she took Lainhart's knobby hand within hers and turned toward Hunter.

The music started again.

But this time, it was Lainhart who proudly held his head as high as he could as he gripped Gwen's hand. The butler pushed the wheeled chair forward. People continued to whisper. Hunter looked to Gwen for confirmation that everything was all right, that she was indeed happy to have Lainhart escort her, a man she knew Hunter did not do well with.

Her smile was bright, her eyes glistened with tears, and then she nodded her head to Lainhart who, with his free hand, pointed at the blackboard in his lap and showed it to the audience as they continued down the aisle.

"My new granddaughter" is what it said.

And Hunter found that the emotions he'd been trying so desperately to keep inside, the ones that had been threatening to overtake him for years, burst free.

And he was again a man broken.

Only this time, his undoing was not death.

But life.

CHAPTER TWENTY-SEVEN

Wolf—

You may be waiting a very, very long time. Perhaps it would be wise to lower your expectations. I know I did.

—Red

GWEN GRIPPED HUNTER'S HAND. It was sweaty and shaking, and then she saw it. If she had been looking the other way she would have never known, but a stray tear made its way down his chiseled face and dropped onto the floor.

And then he turned his golden eyes to her. Their gazes locked and all she cared about was kissing away his pain, of being his partner in more than one way, of being his savior. His everything.

The vicar announced them husband and wife. People clapped, but she could barely hear anything going on around her. All she was focused on was Hunter's eyes. He leaned in and touched his lips lightly to hers and then placed both hands on either side of her face, pulling her in for a longer kiss. It was a branding, a burning kiss, and one that showed possession.

When he pulled back, she leaned forward. He shook his head in amusement and offered his arm.

They walked to the carriage amidst cheers from the crowds. Hunter helped her in. When the carriage pulled away, she sighed.

"So, where are we going?" She hadn't given it much thought earlier, but the last thing she wanted to do was spend her wedding night at Dominique and Isabelle's house! Imagine! Everyone would know, and it would be... uncomfortable. They'd already decided to forgo the wedding breakfast.

"Well..." Hunter grinned wolfishly. "Over the river and through the woods, of course."

"There is no forest, Hunter."

"Says whom?"

"I say. This is London, after all."

"Ah." Hunter tapped the side of her head with his finger. "But where is your imagination, sweetheart?"

She lifted an eyebrow at him as the carriage pulled to a stop. They were at the same house Hunter had brought her to, not but a week ago, when he had tortured her. Lovely. "Last time we were here, you assaulted me," she pointed out.

"True." He grinned.

"Do you plan to whip me this time?"

His half-lidded eyes smoldered. "Do you want me to?"

"Only if I can hit back," she countered.

"But of course." He chuckled. "After you."

Gwen approached the house with dread. Was this his idea of romance? Take her to an abandoned house he hadn't lived in for over nine years? He did not even have a full staff!

Hunter wrapped his arm around her as he pushed the door open and led her in.

How the man had managed to bring a forest into his own

home was quite beyond her. Everywhere she looked were different types of trees in pots, and hanging from each one of the trees were candles in glass jars.

"A forest." She breathed. "You actually have a forest."

"Don't forget the river." He pointed to a small water fountain that indeed resembled a river as it trickled beside one of the trees.

"Why?" She quickly turned to Hunter, hands on hips. "Why did you do this?"

He swallowed and looked down. "When I asked Gwen and Rosalind what to buy for your wedding gift, they said you already had all a girl could ask for."

Gwen nodded slowly. "I still do not understand."

Hunter cleared his throat and continued to stare at the floor. "I got to thinking, what do you buy for a woman who has everything? And then I overheard Dominique and Isabelle talking yesterday afternoon about your love for fairy tales."

Gwen froze. What the devil had they been talking about her for?

"A specific fairy tale was brought up..." Hunter chuckled and raised his eyes to meet hers. "Though the end of that tale is quite alarming. I must say I finally understand how you chose your nickname."

"Red," Gwen mumbled, and tried to hide her smile. "I thought it fit."

"It sure attracted the Wolf." Hunter reached for her hand.

"I assure you that was not my intention."

Hunter laughed. "Clearly. Yet at any rate, you caught one, and considering the Wolf is always painted as the villain, I took it upon myself to clear up the story a bit, do a little rewriting, if you will."

"So the Wolf does not attack the grandmother and Red in the end?"

Hunter drew her into his arms and whispered in her ear,

"I cannot promise not to attack you. What I can promise you is romance. Now, follow me through the forest."

Gwen's heart beat out of her chest. "How do I know that the Wolf is not leading me down a path of destruction?"

"Oh, you can be sure he is, but it will be such a lovely destruction, I doubt you will care."

"Oh?" Gwen bit her lip.

"Yes. I aim to make you forget reality for a while, Red."

"And how do you plan to do that?" She placed her hand in his as he began leading her through the small forest in his entryway and further into the house.

"By becoming your dreams."

Hunter cringed when the words left his mouth. Becoming her dreams? Had he lost his mind? Since when had he started spouting such romantic nonsense? Perhaps it was just his heightened emotions.

He felt completely drained. And irrevocably in love. Which was odd. He hadn't planned for that to happen on his wedding day, of all days. Nor had he thought it would be so swift in taking him out. Wasn't love supposed to develop? Or was it truly different each time?

The way he loved Lucy did not feel this way. His heart had belonged to her, his soul had been hers, but now, as he looked into Gwen's icy blue eyes, he felt lost, as if someone had pushed him from a cliff, and he was still deciding on where his body was to land.

Everything about how he felt about her was raw, needy, and totally ridiculous! But there it was. His heart beat erratically when she smiled at him, and when his Grandfather had claimed her, he had been so proud that she was marrying him that he wasn't sure if he wanted to smile or break down.

"Where are you taking me?" Gwen giggled behind him as he led her through the trees. It had taken over thirty able-bodied men at least six hours to create the forest in his house. Luckily for him, his house was nearly empty and quite dirty already, all things considered.

"You'll see." He continued to lead her to the back of the house, where the ballroom was located. "Just in here."

She walked in behind him and gasped.

He had to admit to being quite proud at his idea. Hunter had never tried to be romantic before and he was so nervous that she would not like what he'd done that he found himself trembling as Gwen took in the sight.

Candles lit the entire room, basking it in a heavenly glow. In the middle of the ballroom sat a small table with a meal. But his genius did not stop there. He had strategically placed trees around the room in a maze. They had to find their way through the maze in order to get to their meal. Another maze led them to the grand fireplace, where he had fur blankets and dessert waiting.

"Well," Hunter stuttered. "What do you think?"

"I think..." Gwen grinned and let out a small laugh. "I think I underestimated you."

"Music to my ears."

"Of course it is." She rolled her eyes. "How do we make it to the food?"

"The trail, you must stay on the trail." Hunter pointed to the beginning of the maze. "And you must listen to my voice as I guide you."

"Listen? Whatever do you mean?"

Hunter pulled out a blindfold and tied it around her head. "The last time you were here, I blindfolded you. I was a cad, an absolute terror, truly you should have shot me the second you found out, so I aim to earn back a little of that trust."

"By blindfolding me again?"

"Yes." Hunter chuckled. "Trust me to get you to where you need to go; trust me to guide you."

"You are asking me to trust a wolf?"

"I told you I was rewriting the story, remember?"

Gwen sighed and then nodded her head. "Alright."

"What was that?" Hunter whispered in her ear, allowing himself to nip her neck with his teeth.

"I said alright," Gwen said through clenched teeth.

"Good." Hunter sighed into her neck. He wanted to kiss every part of her, hold her close like this and never let go.

"Take five steps and then turn right."

He followed as Gwen did exactly what he said.

"Now take two steps and turn right again."

"Are you sure?" she asked.

"Am I wearing a blindfold?" He laughed.

"No." She took a breath and walked two steps ahead. "Now what?"

"Patience." He kissed her neck again. "We need to pause."

"Why?"

"So I can take down your hair." One by one, he pulled the pins out. Her dark hair cascaded down her back in waves. It was heavy in his hands. He closed his eyes and moaned.

Gwen leaned back against him. He flipped her around and kissed her hard across the mouth, dipping his hands into her thick hair and gently tugging.

"Are we there?" Gwen whispered hoarsely.

"Do you care?" Hunter tilted his head and kissed the side of her jaw, then had to touch her lips again. His tongue trailed her lower lip then his teeth gently tugged it and sucked. Her flavor was so unique he couldn't get enough.

"No." Gwen swayed toward him.

"No, you don't care, or no, the kiss was bad?" Hunter

spoke against her lips.

"Hunter." Gwen sighed.

"What?"

"Shut up." Her hands forcefully grabbed his head as she crushed her lips against his. Her arms went around his neck as she forced her body against his. He would happily die this way. He flipped her around and began unfastening her dress.

He fumbled with the buttons and then with a curse finally got one loose. Blazes, how long was this going to take?

Gwen cleared her throat and reached behind her to hand him her dagger.

Clearly he had married a genius. He grabbed the knife and ripped the dress at the seams, not even thinking to ask her if she minded. After all she had provided him with the means to do so.

The dress fell to the floor, leaving yet another battle for him to fight. The corset. Why the blazes did women wear those things?

He sighed in frustration and then pulled Gwen back against him. "I should feed you before I ravish you."

"Should you?" she replied hoarsely.

No. No, what he wanted to do was attack her in the middle of the maze, but he had promised to romance her. Romancing did not include a quick toss with one's wife... besides, he had reason to believe it was her first time.

"Walk ahead three more steps and turn left. It will lead you out of the maze." Gwen stepped out of her dress and walked. He shamelessly watched her hips sway back and forth as she made her way out. Like a lovesick lad, he panted after her and quickly removed the blindfold.

"It's beautiful." Gwen's smile brightened as she looked at the food that had been prepared for them. "But..." Her smile faded. "You are missing something."

"Impossible." Hunter felt panic rise in his chest. "I

specifically asked for a full meal. Do you not care for duck? Should I have included soup?" His hands began to sweat as he took in the meal. What was lacking?

"You are missing wolf," Gwen said simply, and shrugged.

"I'm right here."

"Yes. You are." She beckoned him with her finger. Hunter did not have to be told twice. He took a deep breath and then kissed her as softly as he could. Again, he did not want to scare her. Poor thing was probably more terrified, knowing of his reputation.

"Hunter, stop." She pushed him away and leveled him with a glare. "You promised romance."

"I, uh..." *Eloquent.*

With a grin, Gwen pulled a knife from the table, walked up to Hunter and held it near his throat. "Kiss me, Wolf."

Hunter looked away and then in an instant grabbed the back of her neck, pulling her forward. The knife clattered to the floor. Gwen wrapped her legs around him, and he found that he truly wasn't hungry for food.

But he had planned so carefully, all for her, to rewrite the fairytale to — "Oh, don't stop." He moaned as she licked his ear.

Gwen's nails dug into his neck as she pulled her body tighter against his. He was going to lose his mind if he didn't get her naked. He could see it now: madness by desire.

"Gwen." He placed her on her feet and tried to shrug out of his tight jacket. Why did this always happen to him?

With aching slowness she put her hands flat against his chest and helped push the jacket off, but not before nearly killing him in the process as she kissed and nibbled on his lips every few seconds.

Her hands untucked his shirt and lifted it over his head. Those same hands explored his chest, his stomach, every part of his body that was exposed.

"You are so strong," she murmured as she kissed his shoulder. Hunter felt his chest puff up, unable to help himself. It was what every gentleman longed to hear, *You are so strong, so large, so capable, so sexy, so...* He chuckled and turned her around so he could rid her of her corset. His nimble fingers worked across the strings. Once loosened, he dropped it to the floor, and she stepped out.

With a satisfied smirk he knelt down and slowly unrolled her stockings, kissing the naked skin on her thighs and moving down. He licked the smooth skin behind her knees, and bit along her tiny feet.

Shaking with desire, he tossed the stockings aside and then tugged down her drawers. They fell to the ground, but his hands remained on her hips as he examined her ivory skin, glowing in the firelight. Her beauty was too much — it was all consuming. He closed his eyes and exhaled. Gwen reached down and ran her fingers through his hair and then tilted his chin up. He opened his eyes and rose to his full height, then kissed her briskly across the lips and stepped back.

Naked.

Finally.

He grinned as he examined her nakedness from head to beautiful toes. Everything about her was perfectly proportioned to drive a man insane. And she was all his.

CHAPTER TWENTY-EIGHT

Red—
> *For you... I'd wait forever.*
> *—Wolf*

HUNTER APPEARED NERVOUS AND if there was one thing she knew about Hunter, it was that he was seldom nervous. This was the man who'd practically tossed women's skirts in public and expected people to cheer for him in the process! His hands continued to shake in front of him as he brought each of her fingers to his lips.

"You are still dressed," she pointed out.

"That I am." He smirked.

With a coy smile, she knelt down and grabbed the knife she'd previously dropped. She pointed it directly at his chest. "Remove them. Now."

"Remove what?" He tilted his head and smiled that wicked, beautiful, insane smile.

"Your breeches. Now."

"So demanding."

"You think this is a game?" She grinned even wider and then walked behind him. And held the knife closer to his neck as she kissed and blew into his ear. "I'm not playing around." His skin smelt like soap and leather. She breathed it in, causing the knife to tremble within her hand.

"Oh, but I wish you would, sweetheart," he drawled.

Carefully, she lowered the knife to his pants. He tensed.

"Afraid?"

"You do realize you have a knife closest to what makes me a man."

"Do you trust me?"

"You ask me this now?" His voice was hoarse. She kissed his neck. He moaned. "Fine, yes, yes, oh, yes." He tensed again, this time trying to reach for her, but she quickly turned him around and stripped him of his clothes.

"I mean to repay you for tying me to a chair..." She hadn't ever allowed any of her escapades as a spy to get further than this, in fact she had no idea what she was doing, but she wanted to be owned by him, wanted him to make her his. But at the same time, she had a strong desire to make him suffer.

"I am not entirely comfortable with the look you have in your eyes, sweetheart."

"Rope?" She lifted an eyebrow.

Hunter's eyes widened. "We are both naked. And you want me to go searching for rope?"

"Precisely." She crossed her arms. He groaned his eyes glazing over as he watched her chest rise and fall. "Hunter," she interrupted. "The rope, please?"

"Fine."

She watched him exit through the maze, his godlike body flexing in the firelight. So many muscles tensed and relaxed when he moved; she imagined she could watch him all day and never tire.

Within minutes he returned. "Rope." He lifted it into the air and then threw it at her feet. "Do your worst."

Gwen laughed. "You really should not have said that."

"I do not fear little girls in red capes."

"I am not wearing a cape, nor am I a little girl."

"Believe me..." His eyes caressed her body before he smoothly turned his head to the side and answered, "I know."

She tried to ignore the way his look made her face heat. "Besides, I've never been afraid of the big bad Wolf, and you did say we are rewriting the story. I imagine the Wolf is about to be begging Red."

"I never beg."

"We shall see."

His eyes brightened as she grabbed one of the chairs and motioned for him to sit in it. He licked his lips and sauntered over to the chair.

"Close your eyes," she ordered.

He did as he was told. Gwen smiled to herself, as she felt her body heat just watching her husband sit calmly, waiting for her. All hers. He was all hers.

"Now..." She purred as she approached him and began wrapping the rope around the chair. "Hold your hands behind you, and press them together."

Gwen tied the rope firmly around the chair and then used the ends to bind his hands together. When she was satisfied, she pulled back and grinned.

"Open your eyes."

Hunter smirked. "I'm not yet screaming, Red. Perhaps you are not as good a spy as you originally thought?"

"What? You think all I wanted to do was tie you to a chair? Make you uncomfortable?"

His mouth snapped shut, and he narrowed his eyes. "What is it you want?"

Gwen carefully walked toward him, knowing full well

that the sway of her hips had him hypnotized. When she was finally close enough to touch him, she leaned forward, giving him full view of her feminine body in the firelight, and brushed her lips against his ear. "I want to make you burn."

Hunter swore. His body flexed as he tried to get out of the bonds. Gwen wagged her finger back and forth in front of him.

"Tsk, tsk." She wrapped her arms around his neck and then slowly straddled him. She might be innocent, she might be a virgin, but spying had given her one skill that no innocent maiden possessed.

Knowledge of how to make a man talk.

And even though her own heart was nearly slamming out of her chest, even though her body burned with desire for him to touch her, she wanted to be on equal ground, equal footing. Part of her realized Hunter needed more than a lover — he needed a partner. Someone he could spar with, a person who would challenge him, a wife who would not always do as she was told.

As soon as her skin made contact with his, he let out a long string of curses and closed his eyes. "Gwen." He swore again. "This is…"

"What?" She kissed his neck; he growled in response.

"This is such perfect torture."

Muscles flexed and strained as he tried to touch her. She watched as sweat began to form at his temples, and then he leaned his head forward and touched her chest. "I cannot take much more of this, Gwen."

"The mind is stronger than the body, is it not?"

"No, I say not. Now release me before I die."

"One cannot die from want."

"Watch me." He growled and then kissed her hard across the mouth. His neck strained to push his mouth harder against hers.

Shivering in response, she pulled back, just far enough that his lips could not touch. "How badly do you want me to release you?"

Hunter looked down and then back up. "Do you truly not know the answer to that question?"

With reluctance, she moved away from his lap and began to untie his bonds, as slowly as she was able. When he was free he did not move.

"What are you doing?"

"Counting to five."

"Why?" Perplexed, she walked around to face him.

"Five seconds. You have exactly five seconds to grab your weapon of choice or hide. But know that I will find you."

Gwen searched frantically for the knife. Where the devil had she put it!

"One—"

"Hunter, I think—"

"Two—" He sounded almost bored.

Gwen saw a flash of silver and grasped the knife between her hands.

"Five." He brought his hands in front of him and cracked his knuckles.

"Wait." Gwen held out the knife in front of her. "You said you were counting to five."

Hunter's eyes snapped open. A hungry look rippled across his face as he leaned forward. "Silly Red, didn't you know? Wolves always lie." He lunged for her body. She ran through the trees, through the forest to be exact, but Hunter caught her wrist and brought her backside firmly against him.

His rough whisper sent shivers down her spine. "Have you any idea what I am about to do to you?"

She gulped as his rough hands slowly caressed down her arms and then cradled her waist. "I want you, in every way, Gwen."

"Then take me."

He chuckled. "Oh, I plan to. Remember, the story is being rewritten."

"And how does it end?" she whispered as Hunter began to slowly massage her shoulders.

"The Wolf devours Red."

Hunter lifted her off her feet and cradled her body as he stalked through the trees to the fireplace. He laid her softly across the fur blankets and hovered above her.

"So beautiful," she whispered as she gently touched his muscled stomach. He closed his eyes and then lowered his body over hers.

"Not as beautiful as you."

"Why, Hunter, did you just admit to being less beautiful than another creature?" She laughed nervously as his lips descended and began working their way down her stomach.

"Minx," he whispered as he kissed her navel and then jerked her body up so their chests were touching. "You are more beautiful." He kissed the side of her neck. "More unique." His lips nipped her earlobe. "More desirable." He kissed her eyelids. "Than any woman I have ever come across." The last part he said looking directly into her eyes. The warm golden glow of his eyes seemed to flare to life just before his mouth crushed hers, his tongue begging entry into her mouth.

She opened herself to him — to everything.

CHAPTER TWENTY-NINE

Wolf—
I didn't know you had such patience, though after last night...
I'm yet again proven wrong. Apparently it is not just wolves that
beg, but spies, and Hunters as well...
—Red

THE WOMAN WAS KILLING him. Every touch, every kiss, every caress, nearly drove him mad with want. Mad with passion, with lust, with so many emotions he wasn't sure what was up or down. What his name was, or why he had been so scared to become one with someone again.

A soul mate was just that, someone who saw into the depths of one's soul and instead of retreating, held on for dear life.

That was Gwen.

He nestled her tightly into his body and kissed her cheek. A lock of hair had fallen across her face. He brushed it away and sighed.

He was bound to her. Promised to her. His heart felt as if

someone had taken it and fused the broken pieces together. The fire blazed behind him, his stomach growled with hunger, but all he wanted to do was watch her sleep. He imagined her belly swelled with his children and pride burst through his body.

Home. Finally he was where he belonged. Next to the woman… he sighed as his hand shakily rubbed her arm. Next to the woman he loved.

Hunter awoke to complete darkness. Gwen moaned next to him, and then he heard a door shut. He jolted awake as his eyes adjusted to the darkness. Someone was there. At his house.

He quickly searched for one of the discarded candles on the table and lit it. His eyes had yet to adjust as he made his way through the trees and out into the entryway.

Nothing looked amiss, but the door was wide open. He went to shut it and cursed. As he turned, his eyes caught something on the far wall.

He walked closer and lifted the candle. In blood red lettering was one word. *Traitor.*

Hunter almost dropped the candle. He steadied his breathing and studied the handwriting. It did not appear familiar.

Something was horribly wrong. The only people who even knew of this house or knew he would be here had been Dominique and Montmouth. Then again, he had told Wilkins, considering just a few days previous he had turned in his resignation to the Crown.

He began pacing across the floorboards. Someone must have followed them home last night, which meant they'd either waited for him and Gwen to fall asleep or broken in early this morning.

The clock in the hall chimed six. Well, it seemed his honeymoon was already over. He could not have Gwen in danger. He refused to allow anything to touch her. He quickly went into his study and wrote a note to Dominique and Montmouth, letting them know of what had just taken place. As he finished up, he looked down and saw the packet of codes Wilkins had recently given him.

He lifted the first code to the light and then reached into his desk drawer for the older note, the one Redding had tried to burn, and compared them.

The first part of the note, where it named the location, was in one code, but the word *traitor* was in an entirely different one.

The same code as on the supposedly old ciphers. Which meant Wilkins had given him entirely new ones? What the devil would he do that for? Why would Wilkins give him packets of new codes, ones that had yet to be seen by anyone, if...

Suddenly feeling ill, he took a seat as he replayed images of his meetings with Wilkins, his sudden cheerfulness and changed body language, and then finally the last meeting, where he'd given Hunter the ciphers as evidence.

Why give him new evidence?

Unless he was planting it.

He cursed and ran back into the ballroom to wake Gwen.

The minute he walked into the room, it felt different. Call it a sixth sense, or perhaps insanity or paranoia, but when he reached the fur blankets...

She was gone.

And in her place was a note.

In code.

Hunter donned his clothes as fast as possible. Knowing he probably looked a wreck, he ran out to the stables and saddled his horse, and made for Lainhart's residence straightaway.

A sharp pain inched itself across the back of Gwen's skull. She opened her eyes in confusion. Blurry images stood before her. After blinking a few times, she was able to make out the first person. Hollins glared at her with cold, lifeless eyes.

"How do you feel?" he asked as he pulled a knife from the inside of his jacket.

Gwen glared and shook her head. A gag had been stuffed inside her mouth, so she wasn't able to respond.

"Ah, such expressive eyes, don't you think, Wilkins?"

What?

Gwen's eyes focused on the other figure across the room. Wilkins sat in a chair, a predatory smile gleaming from his mouth. "She's always been hard to tame."

Outraged, Gwen kicked her feet and moved the chair, trying to free herself from the bonds that held her.

Hollins laughed and took a long swig of his drink, then nodded to Wilkins. "How much longer?"

"About an hour." Wilkins examined his pocket watch and sighed. "He will need to take the code to Lainhart. By the time he figures out where we have her, it may be too late. After all, I've been wanting to taste her for over a year. And now that her blood will be on Hunter's hands, I find myself even more... aroused."

Gwen screamed against the gag but the sound was muffled.

Wilkins approached her. His clothes were dark and dirty, as if he hadn't bathed in days. He leaned down, his knees popping as he came to eye level with her. "Stupid woman, thinking she can do a man's job. Though I have to admit to being impressed. After all, you tamed the Wolf, the man who I *thought* I had broken."

Gwen tried to speak again but the gag ate it, so all that came out was another scream.

"Do you love him?"

She stilled.

"Ah, you do! This is even better!" He jumped to his feet and slapped Hollins on the back. "Imagine that! We aim to catch a Wolf and we gain another sad ending to a love story. He shall take his own life the minute he finds out he lost another woman by his own hands. It will be such a tragic tale, don't you think?" Wilkins fingers moved to Gwen's chest. When she was kidnapped her dress from the night previous was discarded. The man who abducted her had thrown a much too tight dress in her direction and ordered her to put it on. It resembled something a prostitute would wear. The gown was dangerously low and of course red, as if mocking what she had done for the crown for a year.

Hollins smirked and tilted his head to Gwen. He was dressed impeccably in tight pantaloons, boots, and a perfectly fitting jacket, almost as if he were getting ready to go pay a visit to someone important.

Who pulled the strings? Was Wilkins the leader or was it Hollins? Gwen's mind worked fast as she tried to put things together.

And then it dawned on her.

There never was a mole.

There never were codes that were being sent back and forth.

The course of the war wasn't at stake.

She looked up.

"Ah, she figured it out. Didn't you, sweetheart?" Hollins laughed. "Too late, though, my dear. Just as it was too late for

Redding. After all, he was getting too close. He accidently took one of the wrong codes and then approached me about a new code, wondering why he wasn't aware of it. Threatened to go above us, and finally took it to Wilkins. Poor fellow. Should have let well enough alone."

Wilkins smirked and patted Hollins on the back. "Now we will wait. The trap is set for the Wolf. He will not be able to escape this."

"No," Hollins agreed. "He will finally die as he was supposed to nine years ago."

Gwen closed her eyes and prayed that Hunter would never find her. She could not live with herself if something happened to him, and she would rather sacrifice her own life than see him lose his.

CHAPTER THIRTY

Red—

For you, I would beg. For you, I would plead. For you, I would sell my soul. If only it meant that I would have you in the warmth of my arms. If only it meant that I could keep you safe from the evil of this world.

—Wolf

HUNTER BARGED INTO HIS grandfather's house and took the steps two at a time. It was early, but he did not care. He'd wake Lainhart up. He'd wake the whole blasted city of London if he had to.

"Grandfather, I—" He pushed through the room and saw Lainhart sitting in his bed, reading by candlelight. His eyes flickered to Hunter's hand where he clenched the note then back to Hunter's face, and then he pointed down and shook his head back and forth.

"N-n-o."

"Someone has taken her." Hunter paced in front of Lainhart. "They broke into my home not but an hour ago. My wall now bears the mark of *Traitor* in blood red. And they left this where she was lying down."

He put the note into Lainhart's hands and waited.

Lainhart examined the note for some time and then smiled.

Why the devil was he smiling?

He pointed to his chalkboard and wrote the word *Easy*.

Well, at least Hunter had that going for him.

Lainhart focused hard on the chalkboard and shook his head then pointed to his empty water glass.

"Water?" Hunter looked at the glass. "You need water to work?"

Lainhart pointed his finger up.

Hunter left and within minutes quickly returned, to find that Lainhart had already decoded part of the address.

After several more minutes, while Hunter was sure his heart slowly died with each passing breath, Lainhart held up his chalkboard.

"Impossible." Hunter shook his head. "No, you see that is impossible."

Lainhart pointed down and shook his head slowly.

"But..." Hunter examined the numbers and street name again. "This is Wilkins' house, this is part of the War Office headquarters."

Lainhart nodded slowly and then moaned. With great effort he opened his mouth and said, "L-lucy K-kill." He took another deep breath, his face turning red from exertion. "K-k-iller."

Hunter's mind reeled back to the original meeting with Lainhart, and then to the packet of information he had been given about all of the men who used to work for Lainhart, including Wilkins.

"Lucy's killer took Gwen?"

Lainhart gave a curt nod and pointed to the address

again.

Hunter's hands began to shake as he noticed the time. It was a twenty-minute ride, pushing his horse the whole way to Wilkins' house. What if he couldn't make it in time before they killed her? What if history would indeed repeat?

He did not even thank his grandfather. He simply ran out of the house and jumped onto his horse. Not caring that he was riding dangerously fast toward the other side of town, but needing to get there before it was too late.

After seventeen minutes of heavy riding, sweat poured from his face. One minute, he had one minute. And then the town clocks began to chime.

"Please, please let me be there in time," he begged.

The house came into view just as the clocks struck seven. A gunshot went off in the house as he ran up the stairs and burst into the room.

Wilkins and Hollins sat calmly near the fireplace. Gwen was tied to a chair, tears streaming down her face. A gag had been stuffed into her mouth, but she did not seem harmed. He could not bring himself to do anything except stare at her. Was it a figment of his imagination or was she truly alive?

She nodded to him. Anger poured through him as his eyes took in her red dress. A mockery, they were making a mockery of her.

He cursed and turned hate-filled eyes to Wilkins and Hollins.

"Bravo!" Wilkins clapped. "Truly better than watching a play. You should have seen your face the moment you barged in here. I thought the gunshot was a great effect, don't you, Hollins?"

Hollins laughed. "Agreed. Now tell us, Hunter, what was your plan? Save the day as always? Become a war hero?"

Hunter's hand flinched by his side. He clenched his fists to keep from charging the men, especially considering they were both armed. "No, I was simply planning on rescuing the fair maiden."

"Not so much a maiden anymore, right, my dear?" Wilkins directed this toward Gwen.

An intense fury burned in Hunter's head, and he stepped toward the men.

Hollins raised his pistol while Wilkins sighed.

"You cannot outsmart us, Hunter. I know your every move," Wilkins answered. "Though it wasn't always that way."

"Pardon?" Hunter sidestepped and walked closer to Gwen, to shield her from the villains.

"Yes. After all, how could I have predicted you would be in the street at the exact moment I tried to murder your brother?"

"Ash?" Hunter felt his stomach drop. "Why the devil would you murder him?"

"He betrayed me. You see, I gave him the opportunity to work for me, to help me in my little smuggling campaign. I aimed to make him rich — he was a second son, after all."

"And he said no?" Hunter suddenly felt proud of his brother. Though he was still a viscount, he hadn't inherited what Hunter had, and their father had only provided for one of them.

"Not only did he say no, but he tried to expose me. It did not help matters that you had already made up your mind to quit. The War Office was at its wit's end to lose one of the best spies our country has ever seen. Their words, not mine."

"Of course," Hunter ground out, and clasped his hands behind his back, dropping a dagger out of his sleeve and revealing it only to Gwen, holding it in front of her face, so she could free herself from the gag and take it with her teeth.

"But things always work out the way they are supposed to. After all, your timing was perfect. Your lovely wife got in the way. I thought you were Ash and when I directed the carriage toward you, she crossed the street. You see, I hadn't expected you back from assignment so soon. It really was so perfect. Ash left the country in grief, never exposing me, for he felt the accident was his fault — and you, you continued to work for the War Office, allowing me to use you as a pawn for the perfect crime."

Hunter's hands shook as he listened to Wilkins talk. How had he not seen how evil this man was? Why hadn't Ash said anything? So many questions that he knew he might not live to find the answers to. Hunter felt a slight tremble through the knife behind him, a sure sign that Gwen was sawing away at her bindings.

He sighed. "Is there a reason for this speech?"

"Patience, Hunter. I am getting there." Wilkins raised a brow and continued talking. "I needed the money; after all, the War office doesn't pay well, and my smuggling business needed a fall-back. Who, other than I, would be intelligent enough to pull it off? Well, of course, it would be you. And who does the War Office have reason not to trust? You. After all, you went off the deep end after your wife's death. Everyone thought so. And now? Now they will see what you have been up to."

"You mean, other than saving lives?" Hunter sneered.

"Smuggling weapons to the French." Wilkins smiled as Hunter frowned. "You see, you even brought the ciphers into your own house. The house that is painted with the name of traitor."

Anger slammed Hunter in the chest. "You set me up."

"And what a tragic little tale it will be! Two of England's greatest spies turned lovers, in prison, set to hang."

"No!" Hunter yelled as the cold metallic knife was dropped into his waiting hands. He took a tentative step away from Gwen. "Not her."

"I'm afraid you do not have a choice. The chess pieces have already been played."

"Implicate me. Take me." Hunter shook his head. "But not her, not Gwen. She did nothing to deserve this. Allow me to take her punishment. Allow me to go in her place. I will admit guilt outright."

Wilkins laughed, but Hollins shushed him. "You would admit all wrongdoing against the Crown?"

"From my very lips ,I will admit guilt. They will not even need testimony nor will they need proof."

"You will hang immediately," Hollins pointed out.

Hunter sighed as he felt the heat of tears pool in his eyes. "My place for hers." It was what should have happened all along. It should have always been he who died nine years ago. Never Lucy. Not Ash. He sighed and ran his fingers through his hair. "The choice is yours, gentlemen. But know, if you send both of us in, I'll use everything in my power to fight it, and we all know I have powerful friends. I will not stop fighting until my last breath is taken from me. I would do anything to protect the woman I love."

"Even die for something you did not do?" Wilkins shook his head. "Well, I believe the plan has worked out to our advantage, then."

Hollins and he nodded, and then Hollins put on his hat. "Well, it seems I have a call to make to Bow Street. Wilkins will release your duchess once we have your hands tied."

Hunter nodded as Hollins went to Gwen's hands and untied them. Hunter bent down to kiss her on the forehead, shielding her body and dropping the knife into her lap in the process.

Gwen jumped from her chair and lunged for Hollins, landing a blow to his face before spitting at him. He fell to the floor with a groan.

Hunter grabbed her and pulled her against him. "We do

not have much time, Gwen."

She turned around and hugged him. Her face pressed against his chest and he realized this might very well be the last time he had her in his arms.

How he loved her. How he wished he could do more, but the funny thing about pasts was they always had a tendency to repeat themselves, and for once in his life he was given a choice. And he chose her.

CHAPTER THIRTY-ONE

Wolf—

What will I do when I no longer wake up next to you? How can my heart continue to beat when it no longer knows the rhythm of its soul mate? I feel lost in the woods and there is no trail, no wolf, to lead me home.

—Red

GWEN GRABBED HUNTER'S HAND, held it within her own, and closed her eyes. Minutes, seconds, tiny fragments of time with the man she loved. And all because of one man's greed, she was having everything taken from her. Everything she cared about, everything she loved, she was touching.

And she was losing him.

With a sob she threw her arms around his neck and memorized his smell, the way his strong arms felt around her. She wasn't stupid; they were not only outnumbered, but she had no weapon save the knife. Even if Hunter did, that meant he could easily shoot one man but endanger her in the process. There wasn't enough time to come up with a different plan other than sacrifice. She wasn't worth it, yet she knew she would do the same for him; therefore by not allowing it, she was stealing what peace he could offer her. She would be throwing his love back in his face.

"I love you," she whispered in his ear. "Hunter, my Wolf."

"Red." He choked. "My Gwen, I love you, more than you will ever know."

But she knew, she saw it in his eyes, saw the pain it took for him to hold her close, knowing it might be the last time. Pain seized her heart as she kissed him one last time.

"Time's up." Hollins jerked Hunter out of Gwen's arms and began pushing him toward the exit just as another figure approached the door from the other side.

"What have we here?"

Gwen gasped.

"Ash." Hunter exhaled, made a motion with his hands to his brother that Gwen did not quite understand, and then ducked as Ash punched Hollins in the face. Hunter returned to Gwen's side and shielded her with his body.

Wilkins was yelling. Gwen looked up to see a wheeled chair appear in the doorway, and then Lainhart lifted his blanket, revealing his hand on the trigger of a blunderbuss as a shot rang out. And then silence.

Hunter removed himself from her body and examined Wilkins. "Direct shot into the head." He licked his lips and then looked to Lainhart. "You shot a blunderbuss with one hand."

"He's a crack shot," Ash answered, hitting Hollins one more time, rendering him completely unconscious.

Hunter stared at his grandfather. He knelt in front of him

and shook his head. "Why did you come? I don't understand?" He looked up at Ash, who seemed to have aged over the years.

He grinned and patted Lainhart on the back. "I've been his butler for the past two months. The minute I heard you were back in town, I returned."

Hunter pulled his brother into a hug and fought the urge to cry. "I thought you dead."

"I deserved death."

"No." Hunter jerked back and stared into his brother's green eyes. "No, you did not. You were doing what was right; you were going to expose him for what he truly was."

"I was a coward." Ash laughed bitterly. "I fled the minute Lucy died. I could not live with myself, did not want to live."

Oh, how Hunter knew the feeling. He slapped his brother on the back and sighed. "Let us discuss it later. Thank you. It seems you were not a second too late."

Ash laughed. Hunter noticed a piercing in Ash's ear and then he pulled back his sleeves, exposing a small tattoo of an axe with the word *Reaper* on the handle. Ash had changed, that much was certain.

"Lainhart woke me." Ash pointed to Lainhart, who was at the moment examining his gun as if he did not believe he was able to shoot with one hand, either. "He began yelling and yelling — moaning is more like it. Finally, I knew something was wrong, and he showed me the chalkboard."

"—Saints alive, is that a dead body!"

"—Devil take me, I need a whiskey."

The noise all came from the same door Lainhart was blocking, where Montmouth and Dominique stood. Both men looked at Wilkins' lifeless body in shock and then back to Hunter.

"How did you know where we were?" Hunter asked.

Dominique stepped around Lainhart and examined the room before pulling Gwen into a hug. "We received a note from Lainhart."

"Called in reinforcements, just in case, eh?" Hunter teased Lainhart. He shrugged and offered a smile before pointing to the gun. "Yes, I imagine you were worried about being able to shoot that beast on your own."

"'Bout stopped my heart," Ash admitted, giving Lainhart a pointed look.

"What the devil happened here, anyway? The note was vague. But it said to bring pistols. I thought I was going to get a chance to finally shoot you, Hunter," Montmouth joked.

Hunter glared. "Sorry to disappoint."

Montmouth waved him off. "It is only a matter of time, I assure you."

"Right."

Gwen came up beside Hunter, laid her head against his shoulder, and sighed. "May we go home now?"

Hunter took a look around. "Yes, I think we should. I have evidence to turn in."

Silence fell heavily upon everyone in the room as they stared at the scene. Two men — one dead, the other unconscious — and a roaring fire, as the morning sun peeked between the curtains into the room.

A fresh start. That was what it felt like, and then Hunter shook his head. "I do not believe it."

"What?" Gwen asked.

"What is the date?"

Dominique cleared his throat and spoke up. "It is May 31."

The anniversary of Lucy's death. Their first anniversary, a year after being married. Either God was insanely cruel or generous, for he had been given a gift on the memorial of the worst day of his life.

"Home," he whispered in Gwen's hair. "Let us go home."

Montmouth and Dominique left with threats that they wanted details of the happenings of that day, or Montmouth would carry out his threat and truly shoot Hunter.

Ash pushed Lainhart through the door and wheeled him down the three stairs toward the carriage, which had been waiting a block down the street. Hunter and Gwen held hands and followed them out, but Lainhart began yelling again.

"Aghhh!" He swatted Ash's hand and pointed up.

Hunter ran to him. "Is it your hand? Did you get burned from the powder?"

Lainhart shook his head and pointed down, then grabbed a piece of chalk and pointed at Ash.

Ash reached into the carriage, pulled out the old duke's chalkboard, and handed it over.

Lainhart stuck his tongue out and concentrated hard as he wrote the word across the chalkboard. Hunter waited, still holding Gwen's hand.

After a few seconds, Lainhart smiled as a tear ran down his cheek. He held up the chalkboard. It said *Proud*.

He pointed at Hunter and pointed back at the chalkboard, over and over again, until he began sobbing. Hunter released Gwen's hand and embraced his grandfather as the old man cried on him.

CHAPTER THIRTY-TWO

Red—

Never again. From this day forward, you may never leave the house. I am locking you in our room and you must carry a pistol with you at all times. Never hesitate, just shoot. I do not care if you shoot into the air when a pigeon scares you. You will protect yourself even if it need be from animals!

—Wolf

IT HAD BEEN TWO DAYS since the incident, and Gwen had seen Hunter a total of three hours in those days. Today was the day the questioning was finished. He refused to let Gwen leave the house, even though he'd allowed her to begin hiring a staff to clean up the forest.

She was, in a word, lonely.

Her sisters visited her often, but her thoughts were always far off, dreaming of Hunter and wondering if things would ever be the same. He shared her bed at night but other than kissing her on her cheek, he did not make love to her, nor did he say a word. He merely held her in his arms until she fell asleep.

Gwen could not help but wonder if he regretted marrying her, or if she did something wrong? Perhaps the fear of losing her had been too much. It felt as if he was pushing her away.

She walked into the ballroom, now empty, and sat in front of the fire, not caring that her new satin blue dinner dress would be crushed.

The light from the fire was all that illuminated the large room. With its impressive ceilings and murals on the walls, it was a sight to behold. She would have never dreamed that Hunter had the money that he did.

But she'd discovered that, next to Stefan and Dominique, he was alongside some of the richest men in England.

But riches did not warm her at night.

She sighed and watched the flames flicker.

"I thought I'd find you here," came a voice from behind her. Instinctively, she grabbed the knife from her bodice and held it out in warning, as Hunter sat down next to her.

"Ah, Gwen, always prepared." He chuckled and handed her a glass of wine. "We have a few things to discuss."

Here it was. Her heart ached as she watched Hunter — her Hunter, the man she loved — curse and run his free hand through his hair.

"Wilkins had been smuggling for a few years. When he got desperate, he began smuggling weapons to the French. The ciphers he left at my house were an attempt to implicate me for smuggling for the past nine years. The codes had documentation of my records. Who had paid me, and so forth. The idea, it seemed, or from what Hollins was willing to say, was that he would decipher the codes for the War Office, they would find me a traitor, and I would be put in prison or die."

Gwen closed her eyes as a tear ran down her cheek. "But why? Why you? I do not understand! He could have placed it on Redding's shoulders; he could have done anything. Was he truly that jealous of you? Or that angry at Ash? I'm sorry, Hunter, I just do not understand."

"And that is what I have to talk to you about." Hunter placed his wine on the table between them and turned his golden eyes upon her. "Ash and I have just been informed. Know that I had no idea of this woman's existence until now."

Gwen felt as if she had just lost all the air in the room as it whooshed out of her lungs. Woman, did he say woman? She felt tears form in her eyes as she watched him struggle to put into words what he was trying to say.

"Just say it," Gwen blurted. "Tell me there is someone else, that you do not love me, but please hurry! I cannot take the silence. I cannot do this! I love you!" Her chest heaved with the exertion of yelling at him.

Hunter's head perked up, and then his lips quirked into a smile before he threw back his head and laughed.

"I'm leaving." She rose from the chair and bolted for the door, but Hunter grabbed her by the wrist and flung her back against his body so she was sitting on him. "I have a knife."

"Then use it," he growled into her ear. "But please be sure to be naked like last time. I found it quite distracting."

She struggled to get free of his grasp, but he held her firmly and chuckled. "Yes, and please with your naughty foreplay."

Gwen huffed and stopped struggling. "Are you finished making fun of me?"

Hunter lifted her off the chair, and while holding her in his arms, kissed her firmly across the mouth, plunging his tongue into its depths. This was no invitation of a kiss. This was not polite — it was hot and needy. He groaned as he knelt down and laid her across the rug, then began slowly undressing her as he kissed her neck.

"I love you, Gwen. I will always love you. I have to admit

to being the worst sort of husband these past three days, but there were things that needed to be settled, and finally I realized something."

Gwen gasped as he bit her lip, then swirled his tongue with hers, and pulled back again. "What is that?"

"It is not my job anymore." He sighed against her chest and began kissing across her neck.

"Because, oh..." She arched her back. "Because you retired?"

"Yes, and because Ash has taken responsibility for... what must be done. I was worried about having to take care of a situation and trying to find a way out of it, but now it seems — You are absolutely..." He ripped at the sleeves of her dress, exposing her corset. "Fully..." He growled as he bit her neck. "Completely..." He moaned as he exposed the top half of her body. "Mine."

"But what about what you needed to talk to me about?" Gwen gasped again as Hunter licked the inside of her wrist and then wickedly began sucking on her fingers.

"It can wait."

"Wait? Until?"

But Hunter had stopped talking and was doing exceedingly well in making her forget what she'd been so worried about in the first place.

Two hours later, they lay in each other's arms. Hunter rose and stoked the fire.

"I am suddenly thankful we do not have a full staff." Gwen giggled. "I can only imagine what a stiff old butler would say to the duke and duchess of the house frolicking around in the ballroom."

"Frolicking?" Hunter paused, his smile making her stomach clench with desire. "Is that what we were doing?"

Gwen laughed as Hunter pounced on her again and whispered, "I thought I was making love to my beautiful wife, but if a good frolic is what you desire, who am I to stand in your way?"

Another hour later and Gwen finally had a new definition for the word frolic, and found that she would never be able to hear it without blushing profusely.

CHAPTER THIRTY-THREE

Wolf—

That was one time! And the pigeon terrified me! I thought it was an intruder! What do you expect me to do? Swat it with my hand? All I had was a pistol. I cannot believe you would hold one tiny indiscretion against me! And no, I refuse to stay locked indoors. And yes, you are an animal. A complete and utter animal, in and out of the bedroom, you scoundrel!

—Red

HUNTER NUDGED GWEN AWAKE as the sun was beginning to rise over the horizon. He had taken her to bed without having a much-needed discussion with her, but the moment he saw the life die in her eyes, he knew he needed to remedy the situation immediately. For it had nothing to do with them, though it had looked that way. He was just so terrified of losing her again and exhausted over the most recent news that he found all he could do was hold her and pray it would fix itself.

For he had been asked to complete a task, something that

246

he could not say no to. Dominique was his best friend; he would die for him, do anything to protect him. And though he wanted to say no, the delicate situation made it hard to. But he could not leave Gwen, so Ash had stepped in, said it was a way for him to redeem his many sins.

Not only had Ash changed from the easygoing brother Hunter had always loved, but he was unpredictable. He would be perfect, that is, if the woman did not kill him first.

"Love," Hunter murmured in Gwen's ear. "Love, you need to wake up. We should talk."

"This early?" Gwen stretched across the bed and moaned. Saints alive, how he wished he could possess his wife instead of having to have such a conversation, but it was necessary.

"Yes, I'm afraid so." He pulled her into his arms and leaned against the headboard while he played with her soft hair.

"What is it?" She yawned again.

"You asked before, why me? Why would Wilkins target me? When he could have set up Trehmont or Hollins, even Redding."

Gwen nodded in his arms; he took a deep breath and continued. "It seems, my love, that Wilkins had somewhat of a grudge against my family, against me."

He grinned and began his story, trying to make it sound as lighthearted as possible. "Once upon a time, there was a beautiful woman. Everyone loved her. Obviously she had the face of a goddess; after all, she was my grandmother by blood."

Gwen laughed in his arms, and he kissed her head. "A man, an untitled man, wanted her for himself. But she refused him. You see, she loved him desperately, but her parents would never approve of the match. So he ran away with her. But her parents intercepted them before they made their marriage legal."

"What happened?" Gwen sat up.

"She married another, and they had beautiful children. Handsome, strapping men, who then had even more handsome sons." He grinned as Gwen swatted him.

"Wilkins was the man?"

He nodded. This was the part he hated, the part that made him sick. "Wilkins was so angry, so bitter over what had taken place, merely because he did not have the station or the money in order to provide for her, that he developed a strong hatred for the gentry, for royalty, anyone in a higher station."

Hunter closed his eyes. "He never stopped loving my grandmother. She would be hard to forget. She often entertained royalty from other countries and on the night of a party, she entertained some of Russia's royalty. Wilkins snuck in uninvited. Grandmother and he had another fight and my grandfather, bless his heart, tried to kick Wilkins out, but Wilkins was drunk. He had a pistol. He shot my grandfather and then shot my grandmother."

"Hunter!" Gwen wrapped her arms around his neck and kissed his cheeks. "So he decided to kill off your entire family."

"No, I do not believe so, though his hatred was strong. I always knew my grandparents had been shot by a madman. I just hadn't known who had done it until now."

"Then how do you know this information? I guess I don't understand. It is horrible, truly horrible, Hunter, but how do you know?"

"He left a book of conquests, people he'd killed, things he'd done. Hollins offered it as a peace offering in order to lessen his sentence."

Gwen held him for a long time before sighing into his chest. "Are you happier, now that you know how your grandparents died?"

"Yes and no. It saddens me to think of their lives cut

short, merely because of a man's jealousy and hatred. I'm surprised he was able to look at me, let alone stand in the same room as me." Hunter swallowed the dryness in his throat. "There is one other thing."

Gwen tensed. "The woman you spoke of earlier?"

"Love, it is not what you think. Calm down before I am forced to frolic with you again."

Gwen blushed bright red and pushed at his chest. He tightened his hold around her and sighed. "Dominique has asked me to go on a mission. A private one."

"No." Gwen shook her head. "We've just been through a mission, and you know I would not let you go alone."

"Don't I know it?" Hunter kissed her pouted lips. "Ash has it in his mind that he needs to do a penance for disappearing for so long, even though he saved our lives. Apparently it will never be enough."

"So he is to find a woman?"

Hunter kissed Gwen's neck. "Not just any woman, Dominique's cousin. I do not know the specifics, but she was forced into hiding. It is Dominique's wish to bring her here and give her a Season, thereby marrying her off and offering her his protection."

"Where is she now?"

"She was brought into Scotland a day or so ago and has been waiting for communication from Dominique, but considering everything that has recently taken place, it hasn't been a smooth transition."

Gwen said nothing for a minute and then turned to him and kissed him firmly across the mouth. "So you are staying?"

"As long as you want me."

"Forever," Gwen whispered across his lips.

"That, my dear, is a long time to live with a wolf."

Gwen leaned back and winked. "I'll be sure to keep my pistol loaded."

Hunter kissed her chin. "Good. You know how I like violence before frolicking."

Another blush stained Gwen's cheeks. "Stop using that word!"

"Frolic, frolic, frolic."

"Sheep, sheep, sheep, sheep," Gwen taunted. "Wasn't that your choice word before?"

"No." Hunter shook his head seriously. "I believe I also talked a great deal about nuts and breadcrumbs. And squirrels."

"You are a strange man." Gwen sighed and then giggled.

"It is why you love me so much. Life is too predictable with other fellows; with me you'll always be guessing."

With that Hunter pulled her into his arms and dove under the blankets.

Another hour later, Gwen rubbed Hunter's back and whispered, "I love you."

"And I you…"

"Good." She sat up in the bed. "Because we have to attend Dominique and Isabelle's house for dinner tonight."

"Will Montmouth be there?"

"Oh, I hope so." Gwen winked. "Perhaps he will get his wish and finally get to shoot you."

"One can only dream," Hunter said dryly, and then attacked his insatiable wife for the third, fourth, perhaps it was the fifth time that morning.

EPILOGUE

One month later, following the Battle of Waterloo

HUNTER GLARED AS MONTMOUTH placed his pistol atop the table, as was his custom every time Hunter and Gwen came to visit. He was convinced Hunter was going to slip up at least once, giving him the pleasure of being able to steal Hunter's life from him. At least now it was a joke, or at least Hunter told himself that so he wouldn't strangle the man. They had come to an agreement of sorts. Hunter kept his flirtatious comments to his own wife, which of course had been his intention all along, and Montmouth would keep his gun out of reach.

Dominique shook his head and rolled his eyes at Hunter as Montmouth polished the gun and then began clearing his throat.

It had been one month since Ash had left in search of Dominique's cousin Sofia, and none of them had heard word about their whereabouts.

"Something has happened," Dominique said quietly to Hunter. "I am not being paranoid. Shouldn't he have contacted us by now? To at least say she was safe? That he had her?"

Dominique wasn't one to worry, but Hunter had the same fears. After all, they had just discovered not but two days ago what Ash had been doing for the past nine years, and it hadn't been taking up the arts of painting or poetry.

No, his twin, his own flesh and blood, had been a gun for hire. To be exact, an assassin for hire. Hunter had even heard of the famous Grimm, for they said every time a mark of ash was found anywhere near a person, they would die three days later, and the Grimm Reaper, or Grimm, would be responsible.

Hunter shivered. No wonder his brother had felt the need for repentance. He had spent half of his life killing people.

Dominique trusted Hunter, therefore Dominique trusted Ash, but now Hunter wasn't so sure Ash deserved that trust.

Gwen placed her hand on Hunter's shoulder and then kissed him lightly on the cheek. With a laugh, Hunter pulled her into his lap and kissed her hard across the mouth.

"Do you mind?" Montmouth roared. "We are eating!"

"I am having my dessert early," Hunter announced between kisses. Gwen laughed as she kissed him back and then the room was somewhat silent. Hunter looked up and smiled as he found Rosalind and Montmouth sharing an intimate embrace, and Dominique and Isabelle kissing as well.

It seemed, in that moment, that perhaps fairy tales did come true.

ABOUT THE AUTHOR

Rachel Van Dyken is the *New York Times, Wall Street Journal*, and *USA Today* bestselling author of over 29 books. She is obsessed with all things Starbucks and makes her home in Idaho with her husband and two snoring boxers.

OTHER BOOKS BY RACHEL VAN DYKEN

The Bet Series
The Bet (Forever Romance)
The Wager (Forever Romance)
The Dare

Eagle Elite
Elite (Forever Romance)
Elect (Forever Romance)
Entice
Elicit

Seaside Series
Tear
Pull
Shatter
Forever
Fall
Strung

Wallflower Trilogy
Waltzing with the Wallflower
Beguiling Bridget
Taming Wilde

London Fairy Tales
Upon a Midnight Dream
Whispered Music
The Wolf's Pursuit
When Ash Falls

Renwick House
The Ugly Duckling Debutante

The Seduction of Sebastian St. James
The Redemption of Lord Rawlings
An Unlikely Alliance
The Devil Duke Takes a Bride

Ruin Series
Ruin
Toxic
Fearless
Shame (October 6, 2014)

Other Titles
The Parting Gift
Compromising Kessen
Savage Winter
Divine Uprising
Every Girl Does It

BLUE TULIP

PUBLISHING

CPSIA information can be obtained
at www.ICGtesting.com
Printed in the USA
FSHW010948170920
73867FS

9 781502 331984